'Charlotte Jay cannot write a dull or graceless sentence. The heroine of *Arms for Adonis*, Sarah Lane, is fascinatingly alive, and her convincing adventures have a background so vividly depicted that Lebanon itself becomes a protagonist in the novel.'

New York Times

'Spirited English lady becomes involved with dashing Syrian colonel; sapphire ring, jewel in tie, musky scent and Turkish tobacco. She sinks, without fully understanding what is happening, into a mess of violent Lebanese politics. A very good thriller, particularly strong in its handling of local prides and extravagances.'

Julian Symons, *Sunday Times*

'Exciting action and brilliantly evocative description of a kind seldom encountered in a thriller. *Arms for Adonis* is well above average in every way.'

British Book News

'Charlotte Jay's eye for the scene is sharp and so is her eye for the attitudes of human pretension. Wryly romantic and a keen delight.'

New York Herald Tribune

'Fun and games throughout in glamorous surroundings; the whole thing is definitely what the *Guide Michelin* calls *Vaut le Voyage*.'

Time and Tide

'The Imperilled Heroine is normally one of the dullest people in fiction, but Charlotte Jay's heroines have guts, and they act rather than waiting to be acted upon. Each is an individual, unpredictably real, undeniably herself and no other woman in or out of fiction. There is suspense and violence in *Arms for Adonis*, and irony and tenderness; and it's doubtful if anyone but Charlotte Jay could have blended these elements so effectively.'

Anthony Boucher

WAKEFIELD CRIME CLASSICS

ARMS FOR ADONIS

Charlotte Jay was born in 1919 in Adelaide, where she now lives after many years of travelling and writing in Europe, Asia, the Middle East and the Pacific. The famous American critic Dorothy B. Hughes has described her as 'one of the most important writers of far-off places and their mysterious qualities.' She spent time during the 1950s in Lebanon, where she set *Arms for Adonis*, a thriller that is alive with the sensuality and political chaos of a land she loves.

Also available in

WAKEFIELD CRIME CLASSICS

THE WHISPERING WALL
by Patricia Carlon

THE MISPLACED CORPSE
by A.E. Martin

BEAT NOT THE BONES
by Charlotte Jay

LIGNY'S LAKE
by S.H. Courtier

SINNERS NEVER DIE
by A.E. Martin

A HANK OF HAIR
by Charlotte Jay

THE SECRET OF THE GARDEN
by Arthur Gask

VANISHING POINT
by Pat Flower

DEATH IN DREAM TIME
by S.H. Courtier

THE SOUVENIR
by Patricia Carlon

COMMON PEOPLE
By A.E. Martin

ARMS for ADONIS

CHARLOTTE JAY

Series editors Michael J. Tolley and Peter Moss

Wakefield Press
Box 2266
Kent Town
South Australia 5071

First published in 1961 by Collins, London and Harper, New York
This revised edition published in Wakefield Crime Classics in February 1994

Copyright © Geraldine Halls 1961, 1994
Afterword copyright © Peter Moss and Michael J. Tolley, 1994

All rights reserved. This book is copyright. Apart from any fair dealing for the purposes of private study, research, criticism or review, as permitted under the Copyright Act, no part may be reproduced without permission. Enquiries should be addressed to the publisher.

Edited by Jane Arms
Designed by Design Bite, Melbourne
Printed and bound by Hyde Park Press, Adelaide

Cataloguing-in-publication data
Jay, Charlotte
Arms for Adonis
ISBN 1 86254 296 1
I. Title. (Series: Wakefield Crime Classics)
A823.3

For Jenny Hayes

ADONIS: A mythological Greek Hunter, son of Cinyaras and Myrrhams, beloved of Aphrodite. He was slain by a boar, and descended to the lower world; Aphrodite sprinkled nectar on his blood and from it sprang the anemone.

He is represented as the type of masculine beauty, and as such appears in poetry. See Ovid's 'Metamorphoses' also Shakespeare's 'Venus and Adonis'.

Everyman's Encyclopedia

CHAPTER I

Sarah awoke, and lying under a sheet only – for it was already hot – sampled the flavour of that Lebanese April morning. She decided after a moment's thought that she did not like the taste of it.

She erred in her prognostications, because she thought the day her own, whereas it was to become public property, her private drama soon to be drowned within it.

Outside, the day was of an auspicious brilliance. The city of Beirut lay like a pile of bright golden stones at the sea's edge, and on the slopes of the mountains the olive groves shone like beaten silver. There was nothing extraordinary about this weather; almost every day in Lebanon touches perfection, and birth and death, festivals and revolutions take place alike in a shower of crystal sunlight. The heavens, in this matter, it would seem, do not discriminate, and neither do the Lebanese, who take whatever befalls them – their troubles and pleasures – with a consistent lightness of heart.

Since the days of Roman Syria, when the city of Berytus became a garrison town, honoured with the title Colonia Julia Augusta Felix and the headquarters of a detachment of the Third Legion, pleasure has been one of Beirut's consuming concerns. Now, practically nothing of Roman Berytus remains – a few stones built into a house in the old part of the town, a broken gateway, granite columns from a demolished temple set into the harbour well – yet perhaps, in spirit, Beirut has not greatly changed. It is still a place where the wealthy come from all over the Middle East for amusement and good living. Night club, racecourse and restaurant have replaced the baths, the theatre and the arena of ancient times, and those native to the city dine and dance and swim in the sea that laps their shores and, like the Romans before them, when the first figs ripen, leave the stifling coastal plain to pass the summer in their mountain villas.

All of which is to say that Beirut can look back upon a long history of gaiety and good living. Visitors declare, after a day or two, that there is something superficial about it. It may be, but there is also something idyllic. And it can hinder any attempt to list its attributes by further contradictions: it is both antique and up to date, floating, with a certain feckless disregard for realities, upon the present but rooted soberly in the past. To add to its complexity, it is both European and Asian and must perforce face both ways – or, at any rate, it cannot afford to alarm its own divided nature by looking too fixedly in one direction.

Such, then, is Beirut – beautiful, voluptuous and gay. It attracts both admiration and envy. Tourists visit it to taste its luxuries and look at its antiquities. Refugees flee to it from the more turbulent and less tolerant lands on either side. The unscrupulous go to it to appropriate its wealth and the covetous, to engineer its destruction.

The visitor, after a week or two which is usually spent moving at high speed from picnic spot to swimming club or restaurant, realises that the Lebanese are afraid, that they wait, anxious and hesitant, in constant expectation of seeing their paradise tumble to the ground around them. Sarah, for instance, who had now been in the country for ten months, had quickly become aware of this nervousness and shared in it for the sake of a people who, she felt, deserved better. But she had quickly adapted herself to local ways and had become used to living on edge.

For the Lebanese take even their fear lightly. They are optimists, living from day to day and hoping for the best. They shrug off the scramble of elections; they are used to a few dead; it always, they declare philosophically, happens like this. The abuse of neighbouring governments, the incitation to murder and violence. What can we do, they ask, we are so small . . . and put up with it. But though cynical and tolerant, they are alert and undeceived by the apparent innocence of an April morning.

Sarah lived in Dhat Rhas, a small village at the foothills of Mount Lebanon, a mile back from the Sidon Road. From her bedroom window she could look westward to Beirut over acres of olive groves. The city was about six miles away but, in the clear Mediterranean air, where every stone looks so distinct it seems precious, it appeared much nearer. The tallest buildings stood out against a sea as blue as the wild iris that a month ago had bloomed on the stony hills. Even in the short time she had been in Lebanon, Sarah could notice here and there an alteration in the skyline because, with American aid and Saudi Arabians pouring money into the place, hotels and blocks of flats were shooting up everywhere – it was said that one Saudi had put up a twelve-storey block of flats for no other reason than to shut out the view from a rival sheik's window. Indeed it had been to escape the discomforts of the new boom that Sarah had persuaded Marcel Gautier to take an apartment in Dhat Rhas rather than in Beirut itself, though Marcel, being half-French and half-Lebanese, had not noticed the incessant din of the Beirut streets until it had been pointed out to him.

Dhat Rhas, between sea and mountain, provided them with the best of two worlds. They were not far from Beirut, yet pine forests swept down to their back door; in spring the scent of almond blossoms filled their bedroom; they woke to the sound of sheep bells in the early morning. Others, like Marcel and Sarah, it is true, had fled from the town and the landscape was quickly being spoiled to accommodate them. Old stone houses were being knocked down to make way for concrete flats, and Sundays were a nightmare of motor horns and the screeching of tyres as the Beirut taxis swooped wildly up the narrow roads; but one could still escape into the silence of the pine woods, and parts of the village planted with fruit orchards, steep winding stairways and stone farms remained unspoiled.

Even now, as Sarah glanced out of the window, black and white goats were nibbling at the new almond leaves in the orchard alongside the house, and a donkey trotted up the road, the bells on its bridle tinkling, and red poppies dropping down to the road from the bundles of cut grass that flopped about on its back.

Sarah turned away from the window and sat down at her dressing table, murmuring admonishments at her reflection in the looking glass.

The glass showed a face which, in its colouring and spirited expression, somewhat resembled a Siamese cat. Fine slate-brown hair cut short; a creamy skin with little colour in the cheeks but of delicate transparency; the eyes large, long-lashed, a truculent blue. The remarkable size and vivid colour of Sarah's eyes rendered them noticeable over quite a distance, and by some purely physiological accident they seemed often to register an expression of inquiry or supplication, so that perfect strangers found themselves drifting towards her under the impression that she had asked a question or called for help. She was rarely allowed to be alone for long. It was perhaps for this reason that she was able to make reckless, uncompromising decisions and carry them out, as today, for instance. Recognising, without conceit, her ability to fall on her feet, she had had so far little sense of insecurity, though her life since the death of her father six years ago had conspicuously lacked stability. But she was twenty-seven and mused that morning with a new sobriety that this kind of thing had been going on quite long enough.

Only a year ago she had burnt her boats – English boats that time – and come to Lebanon.

'Jeanne!'

'Yes, Madame.' Jeanne, a pretty girl, who had been washing the floor with a bucket of water and a rush broom, appeared in the doorway, damp and barefoot.

'Bring me the large suitcase from the back room.'

Jeanne, restive with curiosity, handed out dresses from the wardrobe while Sarah packed them away.

'You are going away, Madame? What a lot of clothes you are taking.' And a moment later, as Sarah pointed to a woollen dress, she said. 'You won't want that, Madame. It will be hot even in the mountains. Are you going to the Cedars, Madame?'

'No.' Sarah searched a drawer. Where was that green scarf. The little bitch, I suppose she's pinched it. Well, I never liked it much . . .

'Madame, are you going to America?' Jeanne imagined the world outside the Middle East as largely taken up by America; a cousin had gone there and married a Greek who kept a restaurant and sent money back to her family in Lebanon. Jeanne had ambitions of going there too with her brother, who could leave the army then and would not have to be killed by Jews, Egyptians or Kuwaitis.

'You are going home to your mother,' cried Jeanne, as another woollen jacket went inside the suitcase. 'You are going away! Oh, Madame!' And she burst into tears.

The silly little fool, thought Sarah. What's she crying for? She hates me. And began to cry too. She's not a bad little thing. I shall miss her. And what a cook. I wish I'd found out how she does those stuffed aubergines.

'Now listen, Jeanne, there's nothing to cry about. I'm going into town now. As soon as you've finished your work I want you to ring up a taxi, but don't say anything to anyone. This is none of your business. Then take this suitcase and leave it at Dobbies in El Hamra – before twelve. I'll pick it up there. I'll be back in a few days,' she said, thinking, better to say that and stop all the fuss. How like an Arab to make your life miserable for six months and then weep all over you when you're going away. Jeanne was not Arab, she was Lebanese, but Sarah was in no mood for such fine distinctions. 'Here's the money for the taxi. Now do you understand?'

But Jeanne was not so easily deceived. *'Oh! pauvre Madame . . . pauvre Monsieur!'* she wept, clutching the note. 'Your beautiful dresses,' she added irrationally.

'You can have those two over there. I was going to give them to you.'

'Merci, Madame,' said Jeanne, quietening down and wiping her eyes.

Sarah was going through the contents of her handbag: her passport, her wallet and thirty pounds sterling in traveller's cheques – all the money she possessed – comb, compact, lipstick, an old tousled letter from Marcel . . . She opened it. It contained little to awaken tender regrets. 'Meet me at the swimming club, 5:30 – Marcel.' Since the time of their meeting nine months ago they had been almost constantly together and there were no love letters to destroy, so Sarah destroyed the note instead, leaving the torn pieces ostentatiously on the dressing table. Then taking pen and paper she wrote to him, swiftly, a dry little letter concerned mainly with salary owing to Jeanne. Sealing the letter she propped it up against Marcel's hairbrush.

It was 9:30 when she walked down the flight of stone steps that led from the house onto the road below. Old Dr Chamoun, who with his wife and married daughters lived on the ground floor, was pottering about among his rose bushes – a tall bony figure in pyjamas and slippers – for like most of the men of Dhat Rhas he not only slept but spent a good many of his waking hours in this attire.

His daughter, who was standing at the front door buying fruit from a farmer with a donkey, called out a greeting to

Sarah as she passed. A handsome woman, running to flesh, she wore a black silk dress, high-heeled shoes and pearls, for the ladies of Dhat Rhas were ready at nine in the morning to receive visits from those of their neighbours and relatives with whom they were on speaking terms and spent a large part of the day playing trictrac, sipping small cups of thick Turkish coffee and passing the hookah back and forth.

These social habits had little appeal for Sarah and she had kept aloof from these Lebanese women; in spite of their elegant French clothes and big American cars, a hint of profitless indolence from the old Turkish life clung about them and repelled her. But they were gentle and warm-hearted; she felt free to enter their homes whenever she wished and yet won no censure from them for rarely doing so.

As she crossed the road and continued down the steps toward the centre of the village, she thought of them with affection and regret. She knew so little about them – an opportunity had been missed, and now it was too late.

The charm of Dhat Rhas, of all Lebanon, for Dhat Rhas might have been any Lebanese village perched up on the terraced hills, pressed painfully upon Sarah that morning. She was conscious of a nostalgic ache for what she was leaving; seeing no danger in it she made no effort to defend herself.

The stairway descended steeply between old houses built from large blocks of dressed stone, the bright golden stone of the Middle East, that devours the sunlight. Bougainvillea, hanging in a crimson arch, flung its shadow on the stairway and, among the sticky, scented leaves of the fig trees, green fruit, though still hard, was swelling.

The stairway turned and twisted through a narrow lane between two houses. St Joseph's, the Maronite church, came into view in the village below. Children wearing black pinafores with starched white collars, each carrying a candle and a posy of flowers, were going in through the gate.

Another Feast Day, thought Sarah, shading her eyes with her hand, for in spite of her sunglasses, the light was violent, surging back like a palpitating force from the golden stone. The young leaves on the vine trellises quivered in the glittering air and the shadows of wrought-iron balconies slanting on the walls looked as solid as wrought iron itself. Below, the small white dome of the church belfry shone like silver.

I shall never get used to Gothic again, she thought. The church, though built quite recently, looked antique and primitive with its straight, undecorated walls, small narrow windows and domed roof. It seemed to embody the pagan temple, the mosque and the church – an Oriental and Mediterranean synthesis. One would not have been surprised to find the red flower of Adonis strewn on its altars or to hear the name of Mohammed called out from the little minaret-like belfry.

The stairway led into the centre of the village where three roads met by a row of old houses, now accommodating a café and shops. This was a busy corner and a dangerous one, cluttered by a pile of stones that had been lying spilled out on the edge of the road ever since Sarah had been in Dhat Rhas, and by the posteriors of a donkey and a dirty sheep, which were invariably tethered to the steps of a grain-shop verandah; people waited here for the Beirut buses and the clients of the café sat with their chairs halfway out on the road playing trictrac and smoking hookahs; every now and again there would be flocks of sheep or funerals, schoolchildren or a political rumpus. But these not infrequent hazards were never anticipated by buses or taxis which swept around the corner at breakneck speed. Sarah, that morning, had barely stepped down onto the road when a taxi filled with dark faces and flapping white keffiyehs shot into the narrow road from the upper part of the village. To avoid it she stepped back into the gutter by the butcher's shop.

The taxi whirled on, just missed the sheep on the corner and disappeared, its horn blaring insanely. Sarah glared after it and shouted, 'You fool!' ineffectually in English. Someone else was cursing in Arabic and she turned to see the butcher making gestures of an unfriendly nature with a blood-stained chopper. The freshly killed carcass of a cow dripped from a big steel hook on the shop's ceiling. She recoiled from it in distaste.

There had been water in the gutter . . . She could feel moisture seeping into her sandal. But it was not water; the gutter ran with blood. Sarah shuddered.

And yet, strangely, those fierce-eyed men, their white cotton keffiyehs framing their swarthy faces, and the blood in the gutter, only added weight to her regret. They were part of a picture and of an ambience of which the sunlight, the old stone farms and the early summer flowers were another aspect.

Take part, take all, she thought, with an odd sense of exhilaration and tolerance toward Beirut taxi drivers that can only be entertained on a day of parting from them forever.

Beirut offered a heady mixture that can seduce the soberest heart. It seemed to Sarah that to leave that day would be like getting up and going out in the middle of an exciting play. She felt cheated of the end.

There was no bus and Sarah waited by the grain shop talking to Mrs Hourani, a plump, harassed woman who had come recently from Cairo.

'How can I look upon Lebanon as my home, Madame?' she was inquiring angrily. 'I have lived all my life in Egypt – my family – for five generations. Isn't that Egyptian? Are they more Egyptian than I am? What is an Egyptian, I would like to know. We who have worked hard and gained influence do not now qualify for the name. They'll say the Copts are not Egyptian next'

Sarah, who was trying to remember what time Nadea Raziyah came home on Mondays, because she wanted to say good-bye to her, asked vaguely, 'Did you get any money out?'

'Money! What do you think we are being thrown out for? They take everything, except what we can smuggle out. And it will be Lebanon next. I said to my husband, "What's the use of coming here?" Another two years and we shall have to move on somewhere else. We should have gone to France. It is so difficult. Now, Madame, your husband is French. Why don't you go while you can get your money out? When the Syrians take over Lebanon, what chance will you have then?'

'I don't think it's as bad as all that. The Lebanese are good at keeping out of trouble. They'll get along all right.' What she really meant was that Marcel would get along all right, would know the right people and be well in the thick of things.

'Not yet perhaps,' cried Mrs Hourani, 'but soon! You don't understand, Madame, you don't speak Arabic. They must go on now just to give the people something to shout about.' She broke off and glanced at her watch. 'Where is the bus? I shall be late for my appointment.'

At that moment two buses, one red, one blue, arrived from different directions. The red bus got to the corner first and the driver, a fierce-looking individual with a large moustache, stuck his head out of the window and yelled, 'Beyrouth! Beyrouth!'

'Not that one,' said Sarah, putting a restraining hand on her companion's arm, because Mrs Hourani, newly arrived and untutored in the subtleties of the Dhat Rhas bus service, was already stepping out onto the road. 'He'll take you halfway up the mountains before he turns back for town. He's only trying to get in first.'

They waited. The driver of the red bus, finding he could not lure any passengers on board, became revengeful and obstructive, refusing to move his vehicle from the middle of the road where it stood, chugging and shaking and blocking the progress of the blue bus. A taxi appeared; horns began honking monotonously; the two bus drivers shouted at each other, then got out and, standing nose to nose like fighting cocks, launched into one of those violent but abortive arguments that are a feature of Beirut. It all came to nothing. Each driver returned, muttering, to his seat. The red bus backed a little, though not so much as to admit defeat, and the blue bus, by scraping its mudguard along the wall and knocking over a case of apples, managed to get by. Sarah and Mrs Hourani got into it and sat down behind the driver, a fat man whose countenance, now bereft of anger, looked jovial and kindly. Pictures of the Virgin Mary, stuck up along the windscreen, proclaimed him to be Christian. A string of blue beads dangled from the rear-vision mirror.

Amber beads for Muslims, blue beads for Christians, someone had told Sarah; blue, the colour of the Christian heaven and the Virgin's robe. But someone else had said that whatever religion you were – Christian, Muslim or Druse – blue would protect you from the evil eye. Houses in the mountains had blue wooden shutters, donkeys wore blue bead collars. It was a vague country. Nobody was much interested in history or the question of origins and, when they were, usually in a dreamy, inaccurate way. Sarah was always correcting Michel Adib, her French professor, when he talked about the Phoenicians or the Crusades or anything more remote than the departure of the French. The present was the thing – the exciting, turbulent present. Politics, not history. The Lebanese could claim so much of history they had little reverence for it: there it was piled up behind them, millennium upon millennium. It bored them.

The blue bus began to move off on its journey to Beirut. It was on the verge of collapse and, for this reason only, moved slowly, shaking like a pneumatic drill. There was no knowing how long it would take to make the journey; if it stuck to its course it should get to the Place du Cannon in twenty minutes, but the drivers had a way of wandering far off their routes in search of passengers. On one occasion, Sarah remembered, the driver, attracted by a crowd of people at the end of a lane, headed his bus into them, crying, 'Beyrouth! Beyrouth!' out of the window, only to find himself in the middle of a funeral procession. It had taken an hour and a half to get into town that morning.

But on this day there was no such diversion. My last bus ride, she thought, as they rattled down the Rue de Damas past the racecourse and the groves of umbrella pines. It was like a pilgrimage. The thought, once having entered her head, fixed her mood. And on that her fate was decided.

The Place du Cannon, that morning, was in its usual state of animated confusion. Around lawns picked out by tattered palm trees and beautified with ponds and flower beds, cars and taxis honked, swooped, backed into one another and rushed for hapless pedestrians. Nearly all the cars were new (few Lebanese cars live to grow old) and large, for the Middle East pays no homage to modesty or discretion; their drivers handled them with a bravado and dexterity touching on the miraculous. Every man made his own rules: to give way to another until the very brink of death was contemptible. Here and there ineffectual traffic police stood gesticulating in a frenzied way and stopping not one line of traffic and then another, but an occasional isolated car, which seemed, through some faltering in the driver's decision, disposed to stop anyway.

Sarah, leaving the bus terminus and entering the square from the top where the little dirty yellow trams rocked along the Rue des Martyrs, felt part of her life was rushing past her and leaving her stranded.

The spasm of revulsion that had sent her fleeing from Marcel that morning had passed, and she walked past the coffee shops and confectioners with their shallow trays of saffron sweets, her head filled with sober thoughts of the future. She was not going to change her mind about leaving Marcel, but the prospect of returning to London more or less penniless was not entrancing, and she walked slowly, hoping that something might happen to hold her back.

Beirut had suited her, had offered opportunities for her easy nature. Her spirit had thrived in its exhilarating atmosphere as her body had thrived in its hot summer sunshine. It asked her to accept a happy compromise; it was chaotic, but lusty and dynamic; order never made for rigidity or dullness and confusion stopped just short of anarchy. It was significant that although nobody followed the rules of the road there were few traffic jams – people still managed to get where they were going and had the added pleasure of being able to do so in an adventurous way. Even the ordinary daily round provided for excitement. You faced each new enterprise, however trivial, with the heat of battle in your blood – parking a car, getting a tram, buying a ticket for the cinema, all fell within the scope of contest. A woman could prove her ingenuity over such small matters – and was constantly doing so.

Sarah though of London and, in no mood to do justice to it, could visualise only fog and taxation forms.

Above her head the sky burned deeply blue; her shadow moved beside her, inky on the pavement. She walked on, passing tall Ethiopians with shining, coal-black faces who stood on street corners selling roasted nuts. The top of the square was bright with cinema hoardings – fat Egyptian film stars ogling from ill-drawn posters. Crowds of idle, black-eyed, noisy young men hung around the drink shops that sold orange and carrot juice, Lebanese girls wearing French and Italian clothes tripped past on high-heeled shoes and, outside the cafés at the top of the square, handsome men in amber robes and snow-white tasselled keffiyehs stared at the passing crowd over their hookahs. The air was thick with the exhaust of cars and the scent of hot ghee, coffee and roasting kebab.

At the bottom of the Place she stopped by the money-changers' and, with a wallet of sterling notes, dollars and Lebanese pounds, felt one step nearer to departure. Her return ticket had not expired.

Now – a seat on the plane, the cold English summer, a job and bus queues. No one queued here. Personal pride would not permit it.

Turning the corner Sarah came into Bab Edriss and made a dash across the road. Here the traffic problems were further complicated by a tramline and crossroads at the top of the hill, where cars, hurtling from four different directions, poured into the street.

Near the French suk service taxis waited one behind the other and hoarse-voiced touts shouted out for passengers, 'El Hamra – service! El Hamra – service!' The airway companies had their offices up a wide street to the left, but Sarah, enticed by the scent of freshly baked bread, roses and Damascus apricots, turned and entered the suk.

It was a small market, a narrow lane between tall houses with smaller side lanes leading off it, but Sarah knew of no place that gave her such a feeling of luxury and opulence, such a sense of nature's abundance. Looking around at the flower stalls, the pyramids of vegetables and fruit, you would have thought that the seasons had been defied, that you had stepped into an extravaganza of the year's productivity. Winter and high summer, the warm tropics and the chilly northern spring, were all lavishly represented, for snow still lingered on the high slopes of Mount Lebanon, yet summer had come to the Bekaa and the coast. Bundles of asparagus, aubergine, and sweet peppers shining like green wax kept company with winter leeks, artichokes and oranges. Strawberries and black cherries proclaimed the spring, and the first Bikfaya peaches, hard but red, nestled in vine leaves. The flower stalls were banked with carnations and roses, and small ragged boys were selling the last of the spring flowers, hyacinths and wild cyclamen that still bloomed in the mountains; at the end of the lane where it led out into the next street an old man standing in front of an enormous pink car held out posies of red anemones.

Sarah, stepping out into the sunshine, was tempted to buy

some. Of all the wild flowers in Lebanon she particularly loved the anemone. In spring the olive groves in Dhat Rhas were splashed with their crimson. They grew abundantly, improvidently, thrusting out between the very stones of the orchard terraces.

The old man bent to the bucket at his feet and, taking out a posy, shook the water from the flower stems. *'Coquelicot rouge, Madame, cinquante piastres.'*

Sarah turned to glance back into the suk. The sunlight, striking through the narrow space between the high buildings, blazed upon marigolds and white daisies. Carriers with big yellow baskets trailed behind customers. A dirty youth with red hair, bequeathed to him perhaps from some Crusading ancestor, stood yelling in Arabic and waving bunches of wild broome.

'Coquelicot rouge, cinquante piastres.' The blood of Adonis, thought Sarah, remembering St Joseph's church, that was built like a pagan temple. *Coquelicot rouge* – the symbol of a dying man whose blood stained the hillsides in the spring.

I'll buy some for Nadea, thought Sarah. Nadea, who looked upon the past, except that part of it which had been favourable to her people, as a humiliation, had probably never heard of Adonis and would much prefer roses.

She went to open her bag, but halted. A man walking down the suk – a typical street Arab with dark eyes, a black moustache and stubble on his chin – fixed his eyes on her with a look of astonishment.

At that second the bomb went off.

CHAPTER 2

———

The noise was deafening. A moment of silence and stillness followed upon it and then, as though at a signal, people started shouting and screaming. Sarah was unhurt, but the noise of the explosion had been like a blow. She felt shattered and powerless; and, although the bomb had evidently gone off directly behind her, she stood transfixed, staring into the suk.

Panic had broken loose. People rushed past her yelling. All over the suk could be heard the rasping sound of shutters being pulled down. One of the shopkeepers had caught hold of a man by the arms and the two of them, kicking and writhing, plunged about, knocking over fruit and flowers. Buckets crashed to the ground, and the white fleshy blooms of arum lilies scattered on the pavement were crushed under foot; new potatoes poured out from an overturned sack; and a child, running screaming into a shop, slipped and stumbled over them. On the edge of this scene, unmolested, one of the carriers was quietly helping himself to some cheese and salami sausages. Then somebody, running out from the suk, collided with Sarah and sent her sprawling.

She flung out her hands as she fell and knocked over the bucket of red anemones. An old man, who had either been knocked down also or was crouching on the ground in terror, crawled towards her, shaking his fist. His face with its dirty seamed cheeks and violent eyes was thrust close to her own. He was crying.

Suddenly she felt herself being lifted up and hauled away. The scent of carnations and burnt explosives gave way to Turkish tobacco. She felt too confused to look up at the man who had taken hold of her, and some strange attraction attached her to the chaotic scene so that she hung back in his arms and was dragged to a car and pushed in. She offered no resistance. It seemed advisable to get away from the suk and she supposed, vaguely, that someone was chivalrously rescuing her.

The car started up; she leaned out of the window for a last glimpse. On the pavement the old man was crawling on his knees in what looked to be a pool of blood. But it was not blood – only anemones.

But I did see blood, thought Sarah confusedly. In the butcher's shop with the slaughtered beast bleeding in the gutter. It's all over my shoe.

Then the car shot off from the pavement and, before she had time to collect her wits, they were careering down towards the Avenue des Francais. The shops, the pavement fled by. People were running, police whistles blowing and a confused shouting, audible in the short intervals when the man beside her stopped blaring his horn, coming from the distance.

Every Beirut motorist drives at full speed, but this was the first time that Sarah had been in a car with someone who was seriously in a hurry. The car, moreover, was the largest that she had ever been in. It seemed as wide as the road. The pink bonnet loomed way ahead and silver fin-like structures sticking out at the back gave it an appearance that was both futuristic and predatory. Inside it was upholstered in black and had every possible gadget, including a telephone. Oil, thought Sarah, and looked around her for her handbag. But it had gone.

'Stop!' she cried. 'Stop! Put me down!' The man beside her took no notice but sat with set lips, his eyes fixed on the road ahead. He looked to be around forty, perhaps less, and was remarkably handsome. He held the wheel with one hand on which flashed an enormous sapphire ring; the other, in the manner of Beirut drivers who disdain to keep both hands on the wheel, dangled out of the window. 'Stop!' cried Sarah. 'Please stop!'

'What is the matter with you?' he said. 'I am not abducting you. I am saving your life.'

'My handbag, I dropped it! It's back in the suk!'

'It can't be helped,' said her benefactor indifferently and swerved to avoid a taxi. He had slackened his pace and, every now and again, Sarah noticed, his eyes shifted to the rear vision mirror. Amber beads dangled on the windscreen. A damn Muslim, thought Sarah. High-handed with women.

'Who are you to say it can't be helped? We haven't got oil pouring out of our ears, like you Saudis or whatever you are. Do you realise you've paid more for this ridiculous car than most people have to live on for years. Put me down!'

'I am Syrian,' said her rescuer haughtily, his voice expressive of all the contempt that one Arab feels for another. Every man in the Middle East is proud to be what he is; to suggest that he might be anything else is to insult him with an implication of the second rate. And though the Arabs talk endlessly of unity, in their hearts they despise their less fortunate brethren for belonging to other countries, other tribes, other villages. 'I have saved your life,' he said, 'and instead of thanking me you insult me.'

'I insult you! You damn Arabs think you have a copyright on insult. Well, we have a touch of pride too, so remember that instead of raving on about your grievances. My life was not in danger and if it were I could look after it.'

He glanced at her and smiled. 'So, an English girl with hot, red blood in her veins. I have never thought to meet one.'

Sarah was angry and disconcerted. She made no reply. 'I shall buy you another bag,' he said, still smiling, 'if the loss of such an insignificant article distresses you.' He spoke

English with very little accent. He glanced again at the rear-vision mirror and increased his speed.

Damn the bag! It had my passport in it and my air ticket to London and all the money I have in the world! Realisation of her plight struck her forcibly. 'Put me down!' she cried. 'I must go back.'

But the man beside her paid no heed. The sea came into view, a blue shimmer dotted with the black heads of swimmers. Here hotels and cafés faced the water and shop windows glittered with polished brass and Damascus brocade. News of the explosion had apparently not yet reached this quarter for, apart from the usual confusion of traffic, the atmosphere was relatively calm. Men in grey suits and red fez hats sat in the corner coffee shop, a photographer with a camera on a tripod trailed a crowd of girls, and street urchins, who would have been the first to show signs of excitement if anything untoward were afoot, were busy claiming baksheesh from the motorists who had parked their cars along the sea front.

The road narrowed. They shot past nightclubs of doubtful reputation and came into the next bay. The sea slapped against the stones of the old wall; a man was aquaplaning in front of the Hotel St Georges, and another in pink shorts and a large straw hat held a fishing rod over the balustrade.

'You won't find your bag,' said the Syrian. 'You can't go back. More bombs may be thrown and you'd be killed. Do you know what it's like? First a bomb goes off and then people start fighting. How much money did you have?'

'Thirty pounds,' she said meekly. 'And my passport and my air ticket.'

'Why do you need an air ticket?'

'I was leaving Beirut this evening if there was a seat on a plane. I was on my way to BOAC.'

'And you say thirty pounds is all you have in the world?' He had suddenly arrested their abandoned dash through the city and now, heedless of the irate honking of motorists behind him, crawled along in the middle of the road. Again he turned to look at her. 'That's very little money. You are beautiful. Doesn't some man provide for you?' Before Sarah could answer, he said, 'Why are you carrying all you own around in your handbag. And if you were going to book a seat on a plane, what were you doing in the suk?'

Exasperated beyond words, Sarah shrugged her shoulders. To relieve her feelings she looked him over with a critical eye, noting everything she found to disapprove of. There was practically nothing that did not fall to her condemnation. The sapphire ring. Another jewel winked in his tie which was in any case hideous. A faint perfume – a mixture of some musky scent and Turkish tobacco – wafted from him. He was the opulent East brought up-to-date. Ostentation run riot. His car: what, she demanded contemptuously, could anyone want with such a car, except to shove other people off the road? She imagined his women, and there would be many of them, dressed by a foremost French couturier, made up by specialists from Elizabeth Arden, but still in purda probably, a purda brightened with rock-and-roll and cocktail bars. Who is he? A wealthy playboy? And what does he want from me?

Again he glanced at the rear-vision mirror, and it struck her fleetingly that something was happening that she did not understand. They were driving slowly along the Corniche. It was more open here – the road wide, with trees growing along the sea's edge. The day had turned sultry, and people were bathing off the rocks by the lighthouse. Fishing boats drifted on a sea so calm their slowly moving prows dragged it like scissors pulling blue silk. Sarah turned to look behind them. A vendor with a flat tray and big circular loaves of sesame bread wandered along under the trees calling out his wares in a voice so melancholy it seemed to mourn the sorrows of the world. A car followed, but it did not gain on them, a taxi – she could tell by the red number plate – with a Muslim driver, for there was a large picture of Colonel Nasser stuck on the side of the windscreen.

'You are imagining that taxi is following us?' she said.

'Who can say? When people start throwing bombs, who can say where it will end?' He slackened his speed further. The taxi gained on them and went past. There were two men in the back.

'I don't want to argue with you,' said Sarah. 'It was kind of you to pick me up and I'm grateful to you, but the loss of my bag is really important to me.'

'What a lot you think of money.'

'One has to,' she replied evenly, trying to keep her temper, 'when one has only thirty pounds.'

But she had ceased to care. After all, what was thirty pounds? If it had been a hundred there might have been something to lament. Now I shall be stuck here for weeks, she thought, straightening up this mess. The British Embassy, another passport, arguing with the airways about the lost ticket. It was too exhausting to think about. She yawned and felt sleepy. The morning had been altogether too much. Leaving Marcel, treading in a puddle of blood, bombs going off, no passport and now this peculiar man. What was he up to? Where were they going? Well, he had picked her up and, short of throwing herself out of the window, there was no way of getting away from him for the present. Sarah brushed dirt off her frock, straightened her hair and wished she had not lost her lipstick. Anyway, I can't possibly leave for days, she thought. I may be stuck here until the end of summer.

'I really think,' she said, 'that I would at least like to report the loss of my bag to the police. Couldn't we do that?'

To her surprise, for so far he had not been very co-operative, he said, 'Yes, we should do that.' Stopping the car he slipped into reverse; they went shooting off backwards towards the end of the Corniche and turned up a side street.

At first Sarah assumed that they would be going to a police station, or perhaps to the British Embassy in the direction of which, dodging through narrow lanes, they were now making their way. But when they eventually stopped it was in a narrow street of cafés and small expensive shops. Her companion got out and opened the door for her.

'Please come this way.'

Sarah hesitated. 'Where are we going? I want the police. This isn't a police station.'

'Please leave everything to me,' he said, suddenly solicitous. 'Your life has been threatened. This has been a great shock to you. You shall sit here and drink a cup of coffee while I arrange everything.'

She submitted meekly. It struck her for a moment as being incautious to enter the small, dark doorway of a strange building with an unknown Syrian, but caution had played little part in her affairs that morning and there seemed no point in clutching at it now. To go on was to face, perhaps, some interesting development in her fortunes. To turn back would merely confront her with tedious realities.

CHAPTER 3

The house they entered was not, it turned out, in the least sinister. A rather charming café-restaurant, one of those slightly dilapidated-looking places where the food would probably be good. They went up a rickety stairway and came out onto a terrace overlooking the street. Wooden lattices enclosed it on three sides, and vines, from which bunches of hard green grapes hung down, rambled on a trellis overhead. There were tables set about, geraniums in boxes and a potted oleander covered in pink blossom. A cat dozed in a chair and a brown hen with stony-yellow eyes clucked and pecked about under the tables.

'Please sit down here.' The Syrian pulled back a chair for her and stood commandingly behind it. Not a very attractive table, thought Sarah, who would have liked to sit near the edge of the terrace, where she could look through the lattice at any view there might be, instead of being jammed up in a corner by the cash desk and a jukebox, which at any moment somebody may take it into his head to play. But she sat down obediently and looked about her.

There were only three other people in the café. A young couple, looking French and fashionable, the man with his hair cut *en brosse*, the girl in a sleeveless cotton frock, sat whispering, their heads close together; and in a corner a man in a grey suit and a fez, who sat alone drinking beer and eating black olives, cream cheese and tabouli from an array of little dishes.

Sunlight and the pointed shadows of vine leaves flickered on the check tablecloths. A ladybird fell from the trellis above onto the back of Sarah's hand. The Syrian went to the desk and banged a bell. He was very tall, she noticed, and ridiculously wide across the shoulders. He seemed to know he was handsome and walked menacingly, like a panther. She watched him appreciatively as he created a stir around him.

A waiter appeared, was sent away and returned with a fat, heavy-eyed, unshaven man in pyjamas, who seemed to be the proprietor. Two more waiters came with a writing pad and envelopes, a telephone which they plugged into a connection by the desk, and two cups of Turkish coffee. The fat man in pyjamas listened while the Syrian talked, and then talked while the Syrian, staring at his manicured nails, appeared not to listen. This conversation was in Arabic, and Sarah could make nothing of it. She drank the coffee and felt refreshed.

She began to wonder idly what she would do now. Perhaps the wisest course would be to return to Marcel, and Sarah was not above giving consideration to this. But only for a moment. It had not been the fact of his infidelity that had angered her, but the manner of it. He had seemed, when they had discussed the affair the night before, to be breaking her in, cynically, to habits of promiscuity that would become common practice as she learned to tolerate them. And now, after the incident in the suk, his appeal for her was even more diminished. It had been made clear to her that she lived in a world where bombs were thrown and blood ran in the gutters. In such a world one wanted someone of sterner calibre than Marcel for a life's companion.

In any case there was no need to turn to him, for there was always Nadea. Nadea would put her up, would lend her money; Nadea would love to be imposed upon. It would be like turning the clock back to her first days in Lebanon before she had been such an idiot as to fall in love with Marcel.

The ladybird took flight from the back of her hand. She leaned back and looked at the vine leaves – translucent, glass-green against the sky. She felt drowsy and happy, yes, extraordinary as it was, happier than she had felt for months. It was a relief to have made the break, so long impending, from Marcel. In the meantime the Syrian was looking after everything. He was rather nice, in spite of his pink car. And so handsome. She supposed he must be a person of importance, at least within the confines of this restaurant. Waiters, at his instigation, were running up and down stairs. Now he was on the telephone talking to the police – she supposed it was the police.

She listened but understood nothing.

He looked up and said, 'What is your name, please?' He pushed across a writing pad and handed her a pen from his pocket.

She wrote her name clearly in block letters: Sarah Lane. An honest-to-God simple English name, she thought with satisfaction. It was good to claim it back again.

He had been watching her attentively but now broke out with an impatient, 'Yes, yes –' and began talking on the telephone again. Sarah watched the shadows of the vine leaves on the floor. The speckled hen, clucking, came toward them. What a lot they want to know, she thought. At last he hung up. Again she felt his speculative gaze upon her. It contained little admiration and did not flatter her. It filled her with a vague discomfort; there was a brooding thought in his eyes that she could not read.

'Will I have to make a statement and sign it or something?'

'Perhaps later – not now. Now you will choose a bag, please.'

She turned and started to see a young man carrying an armful of handbags standing beside her. He stepped forward smartly and put his wares on the table. 'Good morning, *Madame!* We have a very large stock of the finest quality handbags. I have brought with me a small selection. If you are not satisfied with these you can step downstairs to our shop.'

'No! No!' cried the Syrian, looking murderous.

'No?' The youth, startled, blinked his large, long-lashed eyes, but recovered quickly. 'This is Italian leather, Madame, the finest quality. These all arrived from Europe only last month.'

'Thank you,' said Sarah, 'but I couldn't possibly.'

'Please, Miss.' The Syrian broke into English. He spoke quietly and with a queer earnestness. 'I have been the cause of loss to you. If you refuse to do as I say you will humiliate me. Tell me, which one do you like?'

'Well, I like that one, but –'

'Say no more,' he said scowling.

'If you will just let me finish –'

'Enough!' said the Syrian.

The young shopkeeper had discreetly faded off, leaving the chosen handbag behind him. Under the table the speckled hen chose that moment to peck at the nail polish on Sarah's toes. She kicked out at it viciously and set it, squawking and shedding feathers, into some potted shrubs.

'Please don't shout at me,' she said. 'I have no intention of taking the handbag. What's more I am going now – '

The man's mad, she thought. His hands were trembling. A bank of grey pallor outlined his beautiful mouth. She pushed back her chair, but his hand shot out and gripped her wrist. 'You will not go,' he whispered.

'Let me go!' she cried.

To her surprise the fingers gripping her wrist relaxed a little. He leaned forward over the table and said in a low voice, 'Lady, please stay with me.' Then after a pause he said, 'There is something I must tell you. I would have told you before but I thought it might frighten you. I know now that you are honest and brave and will not repeat what I am going to tell you.'

Sarah was not sure whether or not she wanted to be told. 'That's all right,' she said, gently withdrawing her hand; and then wishing she hadn't. All she could think to say was, 'I'll take the handbag if you want me to. But I have no idea what you're talking about.'

He said quietly, 'There is a man in this city who has hired assassins to kill me. The bomb in the suk was for me and, when it went off, I saw you there. I knew that with you beside me he would make no further attack on me. He, and I too, do not want western powers directing our destiny. The last thing he wants is to give others an excuse to interfere, and so not only you were safe; I was too. Will you walk across there and look down into the street?'

The request came so abruptly she sat staring for a moment before obeying.

'Please.'

She got up; making her way through the tables, she came to the open lattice on the edge of the terrace and looked down. The houses on either side of the street blocked the sunlight out; they were old French-style buildings with tawny plastered walls streaked with pale pink and blue where paint had run down from the wooden shutters. Washing flapped about on the flat roofs. There were few people about; the pink car was parked where they had left it in front of the restaurant and one of the waiters, evidently standing guard over it, leaned against the front mudguard; an itinerant vendor selling green almonds and apricots trundled his barrow along the centre of the road. Some fifty yards further down stood a green car, a taxi, with a coloured photograph of Colonel Nasser on the windscreen.

Sarah turned and walked back to the table. 'All I can see is a taxi, a green car.'

'They have followed me.'

For a moment she too had thought this, but the suspicion, put into words, seemed too far-fetched to be taken seriously.

He leaned forward and, with his hand on her wrist, said softly, 'Please stay with me.'

A long silence followed.

'How long do you want me to stay with you?' she asked.

She had expected him to say, Till next Monday, or, Till the end of the month, and was a little dashed when he replied, 'Till half past twelve.'

She looked at her watch. It was 11:30. 'Why?'

'Because then I have an appointment.'

'I see,' she said. 'Well, I don't mind.' She lapsed into silence.

The noise of Beirut – the rush of traffic and honking of horns – came up muffled from the streets outside. But the café was quiet and peaceful. The Syrian had taken pen and paper and was bending over the table, writing quickly. For some time the only sound was the low murmur of the young couple in the corner. The moments ticked by. Sarah became conscious of a feeling of unreality. What have I got myself into, she thought. She looked up to find his eyes upon her. He had finished writing and held two letters in sealed envelopes in his hand.

'Sarah,' he said, 'is a Muslim name. Sarah was Abraham's wife.'

Sarah stiffened defensively. Not because there was any impertinence in his manner, but because his dark, steady regard disturbed her.

'It's a Jewish name too,' she said. 'Abraham was a Jew.'

The retort, once made, struck her as outrageously foolhardy. He'll murder me, she thought, but his expression did not change.

'Jesus was a Jew too.'

Sarah smiled back. 'Yes, but I don't mind.'

'That's true. You English are cold-blooded. You don't mind anything.'

'That's ridiculous. We just don't waste our passions. We make sure that the things we mind about are worth our notice.' A fine one I am to talk, she thought.

'That's true too. We do not always know the difference between important and unimportant things. I have been to Europe. It is easier there. Your history has sorted these things out for you. You think you are wiser than we are, but it is your fathers who were wise, not you. You simply enjoy your inheritance. You laugh at us.'

'I'm not laughing.'

'Of course you are! Yet it is we who should laugh. We have covered more ground than you.'

'So it's all a matter of speed and distance is it? That's why you drive such a big car.'

He scowled at her. 'Yes, for us it is speed and distance. Now will you please see if the taxi is still there?'

Ordering me around again, thought Sarah, as she rose to obey him. She went to the lattice and looked down into the street. When she returned to the table he was slipping the gold pen back into his pocket.

'I knew you were alarmed for nothing. It's gone.'

'Then we can go, but first I must make another phone call.'

Not Lebanon, thought Sarah. Too many digits. The Syrian spoke quietly and gently. What a lovely language Arabic can be. Sweet, tender, lilting. If I stay here – and heaven knows why I thought of leaving – I must learn it. Who is he talking to? I think it must be a woman.

Then she, startled, looked at him, to find that he was looking at her. She had heard him speak her name.

The conversation continued for about fifteen minutes, then, replacing the receiver, he said, 'Now we can go. Will you look down at the street?'

He was not, he told her, going to drop her off at Rue Jeanne d'Arc but at the place where he himself was going for his appointment. He apologised for this discourtesy, but it would be more prudent, he explained, for her to stay with him for as long as possible. In any case she would not be greatly inconvenienced, for Rue Jeanne d'Arc was only a few streets away.

They drove along the tramline past the American University and turned toward Rue el Hamra. They passed some fruit stalls and a travel agency, and turned into Rue Zahle.

It was a short, one-way street connecting two larger, busier roads. Down these the traffic rushed with its usual abandon, but Rue Zahle was empty and quiet. The pavements and garden walls looked white hot in the sunlight, the shadows dark and cool, like pools of water. The street contained one tall, narrow block of flats in the process of being built, with a good deal of rubble lying around it, a few small shops that sold cigarettes and vegetables, and some large houses set back in gardens. Outside one of these the car came to a halt. Through an iron gateway set in the stone wall Sarah could see pomegranate and loquat trees.

There were few people about, for it was getting towards the hottest part of the day. Some children were playing in the rubble by the new block of flats; in the shops across the street a fat man dozed behind a counter displaying earthenware bowls of leban and slabs of white sour cheese. There were no other cars in the street and the only pedestrian was an old man who hobbled along the pavement toward them, an extremely ancient and bent–up figure wearing a long, stripped flannel nightshirt, a nightcap with a tassel and large, floppy slippers.

'Is this where you meet your friend?' asked Sarah, as the Syrian opened the door for her. She could not have said why, but she felt suddenly depressed and let down, as though the day had dwindled into an anticlimax.

'My friend? Yes, my friend and colleague.'

'Another Syrian?'

'You must go now.' He spoke impatiently and his eyes flickered watchfully up and down the street, never coming to rest upon her face. 'Please.'

'Well, goodbye.' She held out her hand. It was several seconds before he even noticed it. A car, ignoring the one–way traffic sign, entered the street from the other end and he looked at this and not into Sarah's face.

'Goodbye.'

There was nothing else to do but go. She drew her hand

out of his and with a queer sense of hurt turned away. All that talk of helping her and paying debts. He wasn't even going to make an attempt to see her again. Just talk as usual; give an Arab a chance and he'd talk his head off, but as for doing anything . . . Not that she wanted to see him again – a flashy Syrian. But she didn't like to feel so damned unattractive. Perhaps he's looking at me now, she thought, sorry to have let me go without saying something. Shall I glance back and see? And let an arrogant Syrian see I'm interested . . . Well why not?

She looked back and saw him turn and stagger, as the man in the car opened fire.

Bullets spattered along the wall and the pavement; puffs of white dust spouted up only a few yards from Sarah's feet. The Syrian lurched toward the open gateway, the gun chattered again, he halted and flung out his arms. He seemed hung, poised in a wonderfully graceful attitude, and then slipped to his knees. Sarah had just time to glimpse the muzzle of the gun drawn back from the taxi window and a man's swarthy face. She turned and ran back.

CHAPTER 4

He was kneeling on the pavement, both hands hugged to his breast. As she crouched beside him, he raised his face to her with a look of agony.

'Oh, my God! You're hurt! Put your arm around me.'

Then he opened his lips and said, 'Ain Houssaine,' and fainted.

Running footsteps stopped behind her. Someone grabbed hold of her and hauled her to her feet. She struggled. 'Let me go!'

'You little fool! They're coming back!'

'He's dying!' But the strength had gone out of her. Her legs felt like rubber and would not support her.

'He's dead!' said the man who was half-carrying, half-dragging her down the street.

She did not resist but looked back. The taxi raced past again and opened fire. The Syrian's body lurched and the taxi skidded round the corner into the main road. The Syrian lay huddled and still. Blood stained his shoulder and his thigh.

Everyone in the street, the children on the heap of rubble, the shopkeepers, the fat man behind the leban bowls, had disappeared. Only the old man who had crouched in terror by the wall was sitting on the pavement trying to disentangle his feet from the hem of his nightgown.

They had reached the end of Rue Zahle; opposite, across the road, was a travel agency, posters and photographs in its window. A young woman with short curly black hair and a pretty, vacant, doll-like face ran out to meet them. Taking Sarah's other arm, she helped to lead her into the office and sit her down in an armchair.

Sarah immediately tried to struggle to her feet, but the chair was so low and her body so numb with shock, she found she could not get up. Faces bent over her; the young woman fluttered about, as soft and ineffectual as a butterfly; a fat, unshaven man breathed garlic in her face; other faces crowded around, peering. The place seemed to be full of people. Sarah saw them, as in a nightmare.

Then someone called out authoritatively in French. 'Get back, please! Please get out of here! She may be hurt.' There was a confused murmur and shuffle of feet. 'I'm sorry sir, you'd better come back tomorrow. Georgette, please shut the door.'

Sarah heard the door slam. The man who had brought her there, the girl with the curly hair, alone remained. The man came towards her – a sunburnt face with earnest grey eyes leaned over her. She stared up at him stupidly. 'What is Ain Houssaine?' she said.

He did not reply, but looked puzzled and sympathetic.

'What does it mean?'

'It doesn't mean anything. It's a place.'

A place? Of course. But what place? Somewhere she had heard of it. Marcel, she connected the name with Marcel. But what could it have to do with him? She tried to think. She looked around her vacantly at the photographs on the walls: Baalbek, with its famous six columns, the high slopes of Mt Hermon, the palace at Beit ed Din, the source of the Adonis River in a wild gorge by the sacred grove of Aphrodite.

'Georgette, is there any brandy?'

They poured her brandy. They made her drink it.

'Thank you,' said Sarah, and began to cry. The girl called Georgette hovered over her, patting her hand. The man stood back, looking worried and grave.

'What's happening?' Sarah gasped. 'Is he dead?'

'I'll see.' He left them. The girl went too and stood in the doorway talking to the fat man who smelt of garlic.

Sarah, left to herself, stopped crying and began to tremble. She felt overcome, shaken to her bones with revulsion and anger. She wanted to cry out against – she did not know what – against the shooting down of defenceless people in the street; against the shouting and bloodshed of the Arab world. It seemed to her that his murder was only one of many, a mere incident; that already that morning three people had died. But when she tried to remember who they were, she could only think of the Syrian.

She looked through the big windows and saw that the scene outside had changed. A siren sounded and a police car swerved around into Rue Zahle. People ran after it. Others came out of the shops opposite. The man who had at last managed to extricate his feet from the folds of his nightgown stood around him and then began to hobble towards the little throng of people that had gathered about the Syrian. It seemed terrible to Sarah that even this frail, unsteady figure should respond to the lure of violence.

The man from the travel agency came back. 'The police have come. They won't let me near him.'

'Is he dead?'

He shrugged his shoulders. 'Some say yes. Some say no. This is yours, isn't it? It was lying on the footpath.' And he held out the bag that the Syrian had given her.

Georgette come back, her eyes shining with excitement.

'Alan! He is King Saud's brother!'

'Who told you that?'

She pointed at the fat man outside. 'The man from the fruit stall. He saw him go past. His brother used to work as a waiter in the Palace Hotel. It's always full of Saudis.' She turned to Sarah. 'You saw him better. Was it King Saud's brother?'

'I don't know what King Saud's brother looks like,' said Sarah, trying to stop her teeth from chattering. 'Hasn't he got a lot of brothers? This man was a Syrian.'

The man called Alan took off his jacket and put it over her shoulders. 'How do you know?'

'Because I know.' She was angry now, which was a better proposition than outrage and self-reproach.

'Georgette, will you make some coffee please?' He turned to Sarah. 'You've had a nasty experience, but it's not the end of the world. He probably came to Beirut for asylum. Some political squabble or sand hill dispute. These things are happening all the time. They have nothing to do with you.' He was trying to calm her by minimising the event, but Sarah was enraged and burst out.

'Nothing to do with me! A man drops down at my feet. Is that nothing to do with me? If I'd stayed with him they would never have shot him a second time. They knew he wasn't dead. That's why they came back. And I knew that was why they came back. He would be alive now if I hadn't left him. They would never have shot him again. They wouldn't dare. Why the hell did you have to interfere?'

Alan made no reply. What could he reply to the gibberish of a hysterical girl? Instead he pulled up his jacket that was falling off her shoulder.

'Don't touch me! Leave me alone! You cost that man his life.'

This accusation angered Alan, but he kept his temper. Her body that had trembled under his hand made claim for some indulgence. Hysterical she might be. She was also deeply distressed. More distressed than she ought to have been; for she was no innocent, he guessed, she was tough and experienced. Even her beauty could not disguise her worldliness.

'I expect,' he said, 'that you have not lived in the Middle East as long as I.'

Choosing to hear condescension in his voice, she cried, 'Do you mean because you've been here for years with your eyes half shut, that you understand more than I? Has anyone tried to shoot you? Has anyone thrown a bomb at you?'

Alan said gently, 'The two men in the taxi killed him. You mustn't take this on yourself or pass it on to me.'

Sarah bowed her head and after a moment said in a low voice, 'I'm sorry. I haven't been fair to you. You didn't know. How would you? I should never have left him. I should have stayed with him.'

Georgette, her brow rumpled, her face concerned, handed her a cup of coffee.

Sarah drank it quickly, swallowing a mouthful of sediment and burning her tongue. But she had stopped trembling, and her mind was clear; guilty or not, she was deeply implicated. The Syrian had fallen victim to circumstances that she was not equipped to understand. But Death, working towards the capture of his life, had unscrupulously used her. If anything remained to be done, any protest to be made, who was there to do it or make it if not Sarah herself?

Out in the street the old man in the striped nightgown was talking to two policemen. She saw him raise his hand and point towards the travel agency.

The two policemen crossed the street; the crowd that had gathered on the pavement parted to let them in through the door and as many as could followed them.

They were youngish men and, like most Lebanese policemen, dark and handsome. The elder of the two spoke French. 'Is this your office?' he asked.

'Yes – at least I am part owner. My name's Alan Crawe. My partner isn't here at the moment. This is his sister, Mademoiselle Qazzaz.'

He ignored Sarah, and she wondered if he was deliberately directing attention away from her. The police received his information in a friendly way. Everyone shook hands, and the elder man introduced himself as Inspector Malouf. The onlookers, who had pressed forwards into a close circle around them, seemed pleased to see that everything was going well and nodded to each other, and smiled.

Sarah's attention wandered. She tried to look through the doorway to see if the Syrian was still lying on the pavement, but there were too many people in the way. The man who smelt of garlic had returned and stared at her foolishly over Inspector Malouf's shoulder. There was so much talk among the onlookers it was difficult to hear what Alan Crawe was saying. Something about someone called Ishmael. The police seemed interested in this Ishmael person and asked some questions about him. But what did it all have to do with the Syrian, lying dead out there on the road? Who cared about him and the people who had shot him? Were they just going to get off scot-free? Sarah felt she could have screamed with rage.

Suddenly everyone laughed at something that had been said. My God! What a chummy little party!

'Is he dead?' she burst out. 'Or aren't you interested?'

Everyone looked at her. Inspector Malouf frowned. 'It is we who are asking questions,' he said. 'What is your name?'

'Sarah Lane. I'm English.'

'Your passport please.' Sarah stared up at him, her eyes wide with guilty surprise.

Until that moment she had forgotten about her passport. Now, fleetingly, she recalled the circumstances of its loss and a premonition touched her of impending awkwardness.

'I haven't got one.'

'You must have one, Miss,' said the Inspector in clumsy English. 'You must have a passport. You cannot enter the country without a visa.'

Children, anxious to get a look at Sarah, had wriggled into the front row. She recognised a brat with red hair usually to be seen hanging about the gates of the American University, selling chewing gum. 'Please send these people away,' she cried angrily. 'I can hardly breathe.'

But no Lebanese policeman minds an audience, and

though a good deal of talk burst out in response to Sarah's demand, neither officer seemed disposed to do anything about it.

'Miss, I have asked you for your passport,' cried Inspector Malouf over the din of Arabic. 'It is not for you to give orders, please.'

'I'm sorry, I can't hear you.'

Alan Crawe cleared the room and shut the door.

'Now, if the silence is to your taste,' began the Inspector sarcastically.

'I've told you, I haven't got a passport. I lost it today in the suk and my air ticket and thirty pounds.'

Inspector Malouf was angry with Alan for putting the people out. He knew that he should have done this himself. But so often when he ordered people around they just laughed, or argued with him, or took no notice, which made him look a fool; so as a rule he interfered with them as little as possible. Now he felt humiliated and so revenged himself on Sarah. 'An air ticket to where?' he said sternly, reverting to French, a language which, he perceived, gave him an advantage over her. 'You think you are going away?'

'I was going to London today. I was on my way to the airways office to book my seat.'

'You cannot leave.'

'Oh, I know that,' said Sarah sulkily.

'Excuse me, Inspector –' Alan Crawe spoke with tactful diffidence. 'I don't want to interfere with your investigation, but Miss Lane has suffered a bad shock. This man was shot down under her very eyes. You can see by the way she's trembling –'

'This is terror, I think.'

'It's shock. There's no need to put her through all this. She was only a bystander. I saw it all through the window. She was walking along the pavement. The man was behind her, getting out of his car. He was shot down by some men in a taxi. She only went to help him.'

'But that's not true,' said Sarah. 'I was with him. I was in his car too.'

The inspector turned angrily to Alan. 'You are lying to protect her!'

'He's not lying! You impute to us too much guile, Inspector, we are only blunt English deficient in subtlety. He didn't see me get out of the car, but I did. I was with that man all morning.'

There was a long silence while everyone adjusted their ideas to this information. Sarah, looking from Alan Crawe's grey eyes to Inspector Malouf's dark brown ones, read in both volumes of interested supposition and felt, to her extreme annoyance, the beginning of a blush touching her cheeks. The younger policeman had seated himself at a desk and taken out a notebook as though anticipating that from this point the interview would be worth recording.

'In that case, Mademoiselle,' said Inspector Malouf softly, 'you will be able to tell us his name.'

'I don't know who he was. If you'll only let me –'

Inspector Malouf held up his hand. '*Pardon, Mademoiselle*, if the question is a little delicate, but this man whom you say you were with, *seriez-vous par hasard sa petite amie?*'

'I was not,' she said coldly. 'If you will let me explain. I was walking in the French suk when a bomb went off.'

'Another assassination perhaps.'

But Sarah paid no heed to this irony. The chaotic scene in the suk came back to her with startling clarity: the white lilies trampled under foot, the shouting, the old man kneeling in a pool of blood. She shuddered, and said, 'There was blood in the gutter.'

'More blood, and yet we, the police, hear nothing of these crimes.' He turned and said something in Arabic to the policeman at the desk, who reached out for the telephone.

Sarah put her hands over her face. I must be suffering from shock. How strange, I feel quite stupid. She could see the Syrian's face, looking up at her.

'No, in Dhat Rhas, in the butcher's shop. They had killed a cow.'

'Another bomb in Dhat Rhas,' cried Inspector Malouf, flinging up his arms in a gesture of despair.

Sarah saw Alan Crawe looking at her; she was glad he was there. She remembered the brandy and the coat over her shoulders and the way he had tried to keep them from questioning her. 'If you'll just let me tell you what happened: I came down from Dhat Rhas with my ticket to book a seat on a plane. I was in the suk. A bomb went off. I don't know whether anyone was killed or not. I didn't have time to see. Someone knocked me over on the pavement. I dropped my bag, or perhaps someone snatched it from me, I don't remember. Then this man who said he was a Syrian picked me up in his car and drove away. I told him to go back because I'd dropped my bag, but he said it was dangerous; everyone was fighting.'

'But you have your bag.' She was clutching it in her lap.

'He bought me this one because I lost the other. There's nothing in it.'

The inspector clicked his tongue admonishingly, and Alan Crawe looked away as though it pained him to see a pretty young woman telling such feeble lies.

'How long were you with him?'

'I don't know. About an hour and a half, I think.'

'What were you doing?'

'Drinking coffee in a café,' said Sarah sulkily. 'And don't ask me which café because I don't know and I couldn't take you there either. I never look where I'm going.' It seemed useless and undignified striving for plausibility; but oddly enough, this, the bit about the coffee, was the only part of her story that the inspector found acceptable. One drank coffee on every occasion; it was the most likely thing to have done.

Suddenly the second policeman, who all this time had been talking on the telephone, put down the receiver and cried out, 'There was a bomb thrown in the suk. At ten thirty this morning.'

He turned to Sarah and smiled. She smiled back. Looks of relief appeared on the faces of Alan and Georgette. Even the inspector softened. Pulling up a chair and sitting down, he leaned towards her. 'Now Mademoiselle,' he said gently, 'please tell me what happened.' Poor little creature, he thought protectively. What great eyes, like a frightened gazelle, hurled from one scene of bloody violence to another – Dhat Rhas, the suk, the shooting in Rue Zahle. She had probably been the fellow's mistress, but you couldn't expect a woman to admit to her indiscretions. Perhaps it would be better to ignore that aspect of the question. Interesting as it was.

So Sarah told them her story from the moment of her meeting with the Syrian. More coffee was brought in to her, for now that it had been established that she had been exposed, not only to gun fire, but to high explosives as well, everyone was treating her with the utmost consideration.

She discovered quickly that she had only to put her hand to her forehead and close her eyes for a moment and the inspector would withdraw any question that she did not care to answer, and replace it with another. He seemed, now, to believe her or, at any rate, to suspend disbelief. Or perhaps he felt that if she was lying, he was not going to contest her right to do so. Everything was going well and this atmosphere of solicitous tenderness persisted until it was discovered that one part, at least, of her story could not be supported. The young police officer, who had again been on the telephone, announced that no one had reported the loss of a handbag to the police.

'But that was why we went to the café,' Sarah said, 'to ring up the police. He was talking for about ten minutes. He asked for my name and address, and I wrote them down on a pad . . .' She broke off. How fruitless arguing. Now if Lebanon had been a British Mandate instead of French –

but what with French muddle and Arab obstructiveness it was a wonder anything got done. Sarah was feeling aggressively Anglo–Saxon that morning. Disaster had thrown her back upon the shores of her own nationality, where everything, however dull, seemed dependable and safe. She felt a fleeting pity for the Lebanese, who, however happily situated and richly endowed, could not count on the blessings of an English police force.

'There must be a record somewhere, unless they didn't bother.' She looked up plaintively. 'Can I go now? I'm very tired and I haven't had any lunch.'

Yes, she was allowed to go, but she was not to leave the country; she was not to leave Beirut. They wanted her address – she gave them Nadea's. And, as she had no passport, they wanted someone to vouch for her identity.

'Nadea Raziyah can vouch for me. I've known her all my life. We went to school together.'

'Who is this woman? I do not know her,' said Inspector Malouf who, having failed to trace any report of the missing handbag, had become suspicious again.

'You don't expect to know everyone, do you? She runs a school. She's Jordanian. She's a very keen social worker. Many important people know her. The president's wife –'

'It seems to me,' said Inspector Malouf, becoming quite angry, 'that you know nobody but Jordanians and Syrians. These people are trouble-makers, refugees from Palestine come into our country. We open our hearts to them. What do they do? They listen to the voices of people who would murder our leaders and plot against us. How is it that you only know Jordanians who throw bombs in the suks and Syrians who smuggle arms over our borders and train rebels to fight us?'

Sarah shrugged her shoulders. She knew many Lebanese. Her neighbours in Dhat Rhas, for instance, old Maronite families who claimed to be able to trace their ancestry back seven centuries, beyond the long sluggish years of the

Ottoman Empire to the time of Saladin when the Crusaders built castles along the coast and on the mountain passes. But unfortunately, they and everyone she could think of except Nadea, knew her as Madame Gautier, and she did not feel inclined to entertain Inspector Malouf with an account of her life with Marcel.

She watched the two policemen get into a car and drive away. Outside Rue Zahle the excitement had not appreciably subsided. Quite a few people stood about in groups discussing the assassination and staring at the bullet marks on the pavement. Others crowded about the spot where the Syrian had been lying. At either end of the street policemen had been stationed.

Sarah was so absorbed in the scene that several moments passed before she noticed how quiet it was in the office. Since the departure of the police nobody had said a word. She glanced up and caught Alan Crawe staring at her with a worried expression that seemed to be habitual. Sarah wondered why. Quickly, and with a look of embarrassment, he turned away.

He thinks I've been lying my head off, she thought with surprise. Well, I don't care. Let him think what he wants to. But she felt oddly forlorn and eager to get to Nadea, who would believe anything that friendship and loyalty demanded.

She got up and said in a formal voice, 'I must go now. Thank you. You've been very kind.'

'I'll take you,' said Alan. 'My car's just outside.' She turned to say goodbye to Georgette, but the telephone was ringing and Georgette had gone to answer it.

In silence they walked down the pavement to the car, a large cream vehicle, with 'Anglo–Lebanese Travels Ltd' inscribed on its door. They had just reached it when Georgette appeared in the doorway of the agency. 'Alan! Alan!' she cried.

'One moment, wait for me,' he said to Sarah and turned back. Georgette, in a flurry of full petticoats, ran to meet him and, clutching his arm, lifted a pale frightened face. Sarah saw Alan take her hand and bend over her while she talked. She seemed terrified. Suddenly she bowed her head and burst out weeping. He put an arm around her shoulders and together they went back into the travel agency.

Sarah got into the car and waited. What had happened? Something to do with the telephone call? The incident barely touched her curiosity. She felt numbed by the continual attack of events and something, moreover, told her that sobs and cries of 'Alan! Alan!' came not infrequently to the lips of this tiny, doll-like girl; from the way she had lifted her eyes to his face it was evident that she had cast him in the role of her protector and probably rehearsed him in this part as often as circumstances would allow.

A few moments later he returned and got into the car beside her. 'Is anything wrong?' Sarah asked.

'No, just a silly mistake.'

But he looked troubled and did not speak to her again, except to say goodbye when he dropped her off at Nadea's apartment. And no sooner had she closed the car door and stepped back than the car shot off around the corner.

CHAPTER 5

Sarah was an only child. When she was twelve her mother had died, and her father, who at that time had just retired from the Colonial Office to take up fruit growing in Hampshire, sent her to boarding school. Here it was that she met Nadea Raziyah.

Nadea was the daughter of wealthy Jordanians; she had been a beautiful, animated, intelligent child, and Sarah had been instantly attracted to her. When she was quite young, she had formed a preference for the unusual, romantic and outlandish, and Nadea, in that company of demure English schoolgirls, seemed to be all of these. The very fact of her having come from a hot, distant land provided an irresistible appeal for Sarah, who felt she had been born in the wrong country and craved the sun – resenting its frequent absence as though she had been deprived of a birthright. She listened to Nadea's descriptions of the burning hills of Judea and Moab and determined that one day she would visit them.

Their friendship had lasted throughout their school days and beyond. When, at the age of eighteen, Nadea had returned to her troubled country they had exchanged fervent vows to write to each other, to visit one another, to keep their friendship alive at all costs. And so it had turned out. They had exchanged letters. Nadea had paid a visit to England when she was twenty-four and, two years later, scraping together the last of the money that her father had left her, Sarah had flown to Beirut where Nadea was running a kindergarten for Jordanian children. She had rented an apartment in Rue Jeanne d'Arc and here Sarah had stayed with her until the advent of Marcel. It was to this place that she was now returning.

Nadea lived in one of the few old Turkish houses in Ras Beirut that had somehow escaped the current mania for reconstruction – a beautiful, two-storeyed building set back in a garden planted with eucalyptus, fig trees and oleanders. Like all the old houses in Beirut, it was constructed from blocks of dressed stone; and an outside staircase protected by delicate wrought-iron railings led to the upper storey, where, in front of the triple–pointed window that constituted its most striking architectural feature, a verandah jutted out, supported from beneath by corbelled stone brackets.

Mr and Mrs Hanouche, who owned the house and lived on the ground floor, said that it had been built late in the eighteenth century by Venetian architects brought into the country by the Emir Bechir. But this, if it were true, which was not altogether likely, for houses continued to be built with a certain Italian feeling long after the time of the Emir Bechir, did not prevent them from expressing a desire to have it pulled down and replaced by a concrete building that would compete in modernity with the blocks of flats surrounding them. Times were changing, they said, and there was no denying this.

A few years ago Mr and Mrs Hanouche used to spend their summer evenings on the flat roof sitting under a trellis of bougainvillea and vines, and looking down over the roofs of other houses similar to their own, to the blue sea beyond. Now, stucco and concrete soared high around them, and their house crouched at the bottom of a deep shaft of masonry. From their roof they commanded a fine view into the flat opposite – a view of untidy rooms, and tumbled bedclothes, and of a fat man who was rarely seen wearing anything but pyjamas and hung over the verandah all day drinking Turkish coffee and eating sticky Arab sweets. The block of flats on their left, which had only recently gone up, had been taken over by the officials of minor embassies who annoyed them by throwing melon rinds and empty wine bottles into their garden. On the other side a vacant block planted with peach trees separated them from the next building and allowed a little sun and fresh air to penetrate their windows, but this small field was an unlovely place heaped with uncollected garbage and rubble left lying around by road menders.

Tidiness is not, as Mr and Mrs Hanouche could hardly fail to observe, a Lebanese virtue, and though the people of Beirut are enthusiastic in putting up and pulling down, they are tardy in clearing away. The city displays at all times an air of opulent disorder with more than a touch of squalor about it. Squalor, not of poverty, but such as one might find in the room of a pampered child where expensive toys are left scattered about and broken. Twelve-storey apartment buildings are put up as a way of tax avoidance and left unfinished; garbage litters marble foyers; lifts fail to work; and hardly a Cadillac is without dents in its mudguards.

One is tempted, when first confronted by this expensive sluminess, to think of the Lebanese as irresponsible people, but this would be far from the truth. No nation that had maintained such a precarious foothold in history could be anything but shrewd and capable, and perhaps it comes back in the end to that Lebanese genius for taking things lightly.

Sarah climbed the stairway leading to the upper floor and rang the doorbell. A servant opened the door and led her into the main rooms, where she found Nadea entertaining visitors.

The big, cool room with its three pointed windows and tiled floor reminded Sarah of a church. Forty years ago Mr and Mrs Hanouche had furnished it with low divans covered in old woven rugs of dim, rich colours, an enormous black cupboard inlaid with mother-of-pearl, a Madonna in a niche, some small carved tables and two excessively sentimental pictures. These things remained, and Nadea had only added some indoor plants and an embroidered sampler.

The four people occupying the room were sitting on the divans drinking Turkish coffee and talking excitedly, but they all, as Sarah entered, fell silent and turned to look at her. Nadea darted to her feet.

'Sarah! I was just thinking about you, Isn't that strange? I was thinking how you must meet my friends, and now you have saved me the trouble of fishing you out of Dhat Rhas.' And grabbing Sarah by both hands she dragged her across to the divan.

She was a tall, strikingly handsome young woman, slightly aquiline of feature, her eyes wonderfully dark and brilliant under low straight brows that lent to her face a sullen cast when she was in a bad humour and a touch of savagery when in high spirits. Sarah could see that she was thoroughly worked up about something. Her eyes flashed; a faint flush tinged her olive cheeks; her very hair, hanging in a dark cloud on her shoulders, seemed to sparkle with excitement. She talked so quickly it was almost impossible to follow her.

'Sarah, these are the Thornes, Nigel and Margaret, I knew them in London. I told you about them, don't you remember? You were away somewhere. Now they're doing a tour of the Middle East. Margaret was simply overpowered by Jerusalem. They were just saying they ought to get out while the going's good, but they'll be all right. The Lebanese won't let anyone touch their precious tourists, you can bet your life!'

Sarah, dimly aware that there was some implication in Nadea's excited greeting, but too weary to bother about getting to the bottom of it, sat down.

Left-wing intellectuals, she decided, looking at the Thornes and wishing that Nadea had been on her own. Nigel Thorne was tall and thin with bony wrists that stuck out from coat sleeves some inches too short for him, and a narrow, nervous face that looked at once hard and innocent.

His wife was a pale, skinny creature with blonde hair and a crumpled, worried expression. She looked absurdly young, and yet old at the same time, as though she had withered up a little in late adolescence, but had not got beyond it.

'And this is David Green who is travelling with them,' said Nadea.

'Hi.' The young man who delivered himself of this greeting was a tall, soft-looking individual of a uniform colour, a pale dull dawn, all over – shaven hair, eyes, skin and light-weight suit providing variations only in their differing textures.

Sarah nodded at him resentfully. Why did Nadea always surround herself with dull tourists? You couldn't get near her these days for the stray Americans, French and English that she picked up, well, heaven knows where; she loved nothing better than dragging them off to look at her precious kindergarten or entertaining them at lavish luncheon parties and subjecting them to tirades against the Jews.

Ignoring the visitors, she turned to her friend. 'Can you put me up for a day to two? I'm filthy and destitute. I lost my money and my passport in the French suk. Someone threw a bomb –'

'The bomb! My God! Sarah darling, were you there? Of course! You can have my bed. I'm going to Amman tonight. I must say,' she said, addressing the Thornes, 'we do seem to be turning things on for you: the police at Sofar; bombs in the suk; the Egyptian ambassador murdered under our very eyes.'

'Who?' cried Sarah.

'Do you mean to say you haven't heard?' Nadea was getting more and more excited. 'The Egyptian ambassador has been murdered by government agents. It happened just down here in Rue Zahle, only half an hour ago. I knew there'd be trouble as soon as that so-called American aid mission turned up. There'll be war. The British will come back like a shot into the canal, and that'll bring the Russians in, and that'll bring the Americans. Why these damned people can't mind their own business and leave us alone –'

Everyone looked extremely grave except Nadea, to whom the prospect of these disasters was not, apparently, entirely unpleasing.

Sarah, forgetting her weariness, leaned forward. 'Nadea! Where did you hear all this?'

'It's true, I tell you!' cried Nadea, her eyes glazed with the intoxication of impending calamity. 'Everyone knows it. He was shot down in Rue Zahle. The police let the murderers get away.'

'For God's sake, Nadea,' said Sarah furiously. 'Don't be such a fool and calm down. Use your head. Would the Lebanese be likely to shoot down the Egyptian ambassador? They're trying to live with the Egyptians, heaven help them, they're in a very delicate position, what with the refugee camps and Nasser whipping up all the Moslems. It's the very last thing they'd do.'

'They say the Syrians did it,' cried Nadea excitedly. 'There was a woman with them too. They nearly got her. Everyone knows about it.'

'Everyone, who's everyone?' shouted Sarah. 'You're an educated woman, but when it comes to this sort of thing you'll believe anything. You listen to that demented twaddle on Radio Cairo: three million Chinese marching over Asia to help their Arab brothers –' She broke off. That had been unkind, taunting Nadea with past foolishness; during a time of recent crisis she had so fallen under the spell of Egyptian propaganda as to believe in miracles. But for some reason it made Sarah furiously angry to hear Nadea declare that the Syrian had been the Egyptian ambassador. Everyone, it seemed, cast the Syrian in the role they wanted him to play. Why did Nadea want him to play this one? 'I know a man's been killed,' she said flatly. 'But he wasn't even Egyptian to begin with.'

'How do you know?'

Everyone was looking at her, and it was strange, but she was suddenly reluctant to explain again that she had known the Syrian, and how it was that she had come to know him. I'll tell Nadea when we're alone, she thought. But perhaps she would not even do that. Perhaps she would not tell anyone else at all. Her brief friendship with the Syrian had suddenly become very personal. She did not want people smirching it with their suppositions and disbelief.

'I was going past Rue Zahle on my way here,' she said. 'The police were there; they don't even know who he was. There were the wildest rumours. It's just Beirut. And you hysterical Arabs,' she added spitefully. And then to change the subject, 'Have you got anything for me to eat? I'm famished.'

'Of course! Poor Sarah!' cried Nadea, all remorse and tenderness. 'We've just finished, and I didn't think to offer you anything. You poor thing, and someone threw a bomb at you! Some coffee?'

'There you go again. I didn't say that anyone threw a bomb at me. Have you absolutely no respect for the truth? Must you distort the very simplest statement? And no coffee. I'm pickled in coffee. Food.'

Nadea hurried off.

A brief silence ensued. Then Margaret Thorne said in a low, anxious voice, 'Nigel, I really do think we should seriously consider whether it's wise to go on.'

'Oh, don't worry,' said Sarah angrily, for she was still annoyed with Nadea, 'it's always like this. These people live in a state of permanent hysteria. They can't bear not to be fuming over their grievances. Don't think they want them settled, they couldn't live without them. They've got more now than they've had for ages and they're having the time of their lives.'

Nigel looked at her with cold indignation.

'I had no idea,' said Margaret, pursuing her own thoughts. 'I thought that Beirut would be different, but everyone looks so wild and murderous. The taxi drivers, even Nadea, she's so different here, so much more excitable. There's such a feeling of tension. And all in one day, a man shot in the street, and you say there was a bomb, and we nearly get put in jail, and Jerusalem –' She shuddered. Jerusalem had terrified her. The beautiful lion–coloured city set on its barren hills had seemed so grim and implacably cruel. The prison–like walls, the stark, naked hills. All the trees had been cut down, Nigel had told her, to make crosses for the Jews when Titus and his armies were besieging the city. She could well believe it. She could imagine that forest of crucifixes. All the tragic history of Jerusalem spoke from its golden stones. Intolerance and hatred. They had walked through the suks, and the city had seemed to close around her, even the sky; an appalling fear had come over her that she had been gulped down into the belly of a revengeful beast, and that she would never get out again. And then, to crown it all, a man – and she did not know whether it was by mistake or on purpose – had spat on her leg. When they got back to the hotel she had scrubbed and scrubbed with soap and a nail brush, but somehow the place never seemed to get clean. Whenever she thought of it she felt sick.

'When were you nearly put in jail?' asked Sarah. At that moment Nadea came back in to the room, followed by a servant bringing leban, homus, black olives and Arab bread. 'That's what I was telling you,' she cried. 'They were arrested for subversive activities. Go on, tell us, Margaret, only you'll have to start again.'

The Thornes had met David Green in Jerusalem. They were on their honeymoon, a fact which they had not confessed to him and which they were so careful to conceal that most people took them for brother and sister. The fact of the matter was they both felt rather let down by marriage and were glad to have someone else with them. They had met when Nigel was at Oxford, and both looked back nostalgically to the days when they had been good companions, interested in each other's ideas, and had not had to bother with fumbling around in bed.

And the trip itself, quite apart from their personal difficulties, had not come up to expectations. Margaret had not liked Jordan; the landscape which had entranced Sarah, had little appeal for her, and of the people she was frankly terrified. Nigel fared better. He belonged to a class of English intellectual who, though they have no political allegiance and subscribe to no faith, cling to one idea with burning fervour – the notion of Great Britain's monstrous culpability in the field of international affairs.

This feeling of guilt was for him a voluptuous, ecstatic experience, and nowhere could it be indulged in more happily than in the Middle East, where so much that was distressing to the humanitarian mind – the refugee camps in the Jordan valley, the devastated areas of Jerusalem where Jew had murdered Arab and Arab had murdered Jew, even purdah, beggars and the suspicions of the Syrian customs officials – could, if one felt so inclined, be laid at the door of British imperialism.

He won popularity by expressing, wherever possible, his feeling of responsibility for these various evils and one of the reasons he liked David Green was that the young American was so eager to agree with him. On the whole, if it hadn't been for Margaret, he would have enjoyed himself. But her uneasiness was a reproach to him; he didn't know how to deal with her. It was bad enough that she had been sexually unresponsive – and Nigel was not so much in love with humiliation as to accept any blame for this – but, more seriously, a mental barrier had arisen between them.

Every now and again she would burst out with some remark – some sharp intolerant judgement on the people around her – which coming from anyone else would have enraged him. He was able to be indulgent with her only because he knew perfectly well she did not believe what she was saying; but in that case, he asked himself, why say it?

The Margaret he had known before marriage had been an honest forthright young woman with a personality that had seemed as clear as crystal. And all of a sudden she had become opaque, inconsistent, obtuse.

From Jordan they went to Syria, but Damascus, a touchy, brooding city, had troubled Margaret no less than Jerusalem. Nigel had been relieved when the day arrived for their departure for Lebanon. David Green, who was on holiday from a technical job in Turkey, had been to Beirut before and said that it was quite different from either Jordan and Syria – more like the south of France. And even Sir Richard Burton, whose *Guide Book to Mecca*, along with *Arabia Deserta*, *The Seven Pillars of Wisdom*, and *A Short History of the Middle East*, he carried around with him, had written around 1865, 'Good men will not change civilised Bayrut for dangerous Damascus.'

They had left Damascus early, expecting to arrive in Beirut about ten. They were travelling in a large hired car; the Thornes and David Green sat in the back. In front of them were two Germans who spoke to no one but each other, for they understood no English or French, and a handsome and excitable Iranian journalist who kept looking for and pointing out evidence of the oppressive policies of the French. In the front seat sat the driver, of whom nobody to begin with took much notice, and beside him a representative of the tourist company that had arranged their transport, a plumpish young man with a pleasant, friendly personality who had spent some years in London and spoke fluent English in the way he thought it had been spoken there.

They had been pleased to leave Damascus, and everything, to begin with, went well. They had anticipated a long disagreeable delay at the frontier, the Syrian authorities having already raised strong objections to David Green on the grounds of his Christian name, which rang in their ears with ominous Jewish overtones. But their guide told them there would be no trouble – he and his company were well known to the frontier police – and as he predicted they sailed through the frontier with a minimum of fuss, which put everyone in a good humour.

When they passed through the barren, waterless valleys of the anti-Lebanon and had descended into the Beka'a, their spirits rose higher. The broad green valley stretched away to north and south and, in front of them, surprisingly near, the long range of the Lebanon rose up like a barrier. These are extraordinary mountains, appearing from over the Beka'a both massive and delicate, their lower slopes intricately folded and pierced by innumerable valleys, their crests glittering with snow – not the abundant whiteness of winter, this had melted away – but summer snow like veins of silver struck down between the naked grey ridges.

Those who had not seen this splendid range before, gasped and exclaimed. They crossed the Beka'a, at everyone's request, slowly, for the better enjoyment of all the beauty around them. Fields of green wheat stretched away on either side, red tulips grew among the wheat, and asphodel, blooming in thick clumps at the side of the road, shone in the sunlight like tall spikes of silver.

Everyone talked excitedly about the things they were passing, and the Iranian, who had been jotting down his impressions in a black pocket–book, put this volume away and began to sing wild little songs in his native tongue. The guide pointed out Bedouins with herds of camels and donkeys grazing near their black goat–hair tents; they saw a man in billowing tan robes riding a white mare with red tassels on her bridle and a foal trotting at her heels. They crossed the Litani River under a shimmer of poplar leaves. The air they breathed was heady and scented with the sweet smell of hot grass and flowers and the cold smell of snow. Then they reached Chatuara and began the long climb up the mountains.

At first the Thornes were delighted by the abrupt and dramatic change. The white-washed mud houses of the

Beka'a gave way to stone farms built on the steep terraced hillsides, and instead of camels and sheep there were black and white goats poised on crags or standing on their hind legs pulling at thorn bushes. The lower slopes were warm with sunshine; rocks and stones shone blinding white in the thin, clear air and almond and peach trees putting out new leaf trembled and shimmered as though green water was netted in their branches. But as they mounted higher the mood of the landscape became sad and threatening; huge ash-grey clouds moved swiftly down the mountain slopes blotting out the road ahead.

There were no houses and few cars on the road. A dirty bus crawled up the steep slope, clouds of black smoke pouring from its exhaust. As they went higher, the mist thickened. The posts at the side of the road, grey boulders, thorn bushes, and almond trees black and twisted like corroded iron, appeared like spectres. A shepherd in a white keffiyeh and baggy trousers stood watching over them, a ghostly figure with the mist whirling around him.

Suddenly the mist cleared, at least enough for them to see a few hundred yards ahead. They turned a corner, the road flattened out in front of them; fifty yards ahead by a large grey boulder stood a car and half a dozen policemen. One of these stepped out into the middle of the road and hailed them.

Apparently their guide had not expected this; he was obviously annoyed and, as they drew up began talking to the driver in excited Arabic.

'Why do we stop here?' asked Margaret, instantly apprehensive. 'What do they want?'

'Madam, I don't know.' He fluttered his hands distractedly. 'These fellows never stop us. This is some new ridiculous formality, and I'm jolly well going to kick up hell about it when I get to Beirut.'

The car stopped. He got out and flung himself belligerently into argument with the policeman who had hailed them.

The driver got out too and the discussion warmed up. Two more policemen joined the first so that the guide and the driver were now outnumbered three to two. The talk got louder, gestures freer. The passengers in the car watched anxiously.

At length the guide hunched his shoulders, lifted both hands out from his body and let them fall with a flap to his sides, a gesture eloquently descriptive of exasperated acquiescence. The three policemen walked round to the back of the car and began to pull the luggage off the top. A moment later their guide stuck his head through the window and said in a voice that trembled with anger, 'Would you like to hop out for a minute and stretch your legs? These idiots are insisting on searching your baggage. There's been some smuggling – hashish, this and that. Please don't imagine that this will ever happen again. I'm going to tear such strips off these chaps when I get to Beirut.' He broke off, stuttering, and hurried away.

They all decided to get out. The Germans stood by the car, smoking and watching the police. The Thornes, David and the Iranian walked a few yards down the road and stood looking into the valley. The Iranian, who carried a shooting stick, jabbed the point of this into the turf and sat on it.

'Look at this road that the French built,' he said, addressing himself to Nigel and pointing to the Damascus road winding away down the mountain, till the mist hid it from view. 'But look down there!' He flung out an arm to a little group of farms huddled on the stony hillside below them. 'Did they build roads for those poor people down there? No! They expect them to climb all over the mountain like goats, but they build roads for their own big cars to go back and forth. You see that stone?' Nigel looked obediently. 'That is a Frenchman!' cried the Iranian and, clearing his throat, spat at it with an accuracy that spoke of long practice.

Nigel laughed politely, though with a certain reserve. Margaret walked a little further on and stood looking down into the valley. The hillside, a barren rocky incline dotted with thorn bushes and wild lavender, swept down precipitously towards the little settlement that the Iranian had pointed out. A few acres of land around each farm house had been terraced for orchards, the land refashioned and built up patiently, stone by stone. From where she stood, the terracing, a series of undulating lines carved on the hillside and following the contour of the land, looked like the ridges that the sea makes when it washes against a shelf of sand; and the orchard trees, small and fragile green twigs, stuck out in rows as a child might make a garden.

Nigel came up and stood beside her. 'Quite a drop down there,' he said cheerfully. He had noticed the queer, worried look on her face.

'I hate him,' she said in a low voice, 'I hate him! I bet nobody built roads in his country!'

She was trembling; a most extraordinary impulse had gripped her to pick up a stone, and there were plenty about, and hit the Iranian on the head with it. 'Why does he hate the French, anyway? Iranians are supposed to hate the British! Why don't they work a bit like we've had to do instead of sitting around on shooting sticks blaming other people? I'm sick of hearing all this! I'm sick of it!'

Nigel felt himself becoming angry, but he could see that she was in no mood to be reasonable and answered gently, flattering her with a reference to those liberal views she had once entertained and that seemed to have withered somewhat in the heady Middle Eastern air: 'Surely, you don't need to be told to be patient and have a little understanding.'

She turned on him, almost savagely. 'Why should I? I'm not patient with you or my father or my sister. Why should I be patient with him? It's all hypocrisy, this understanding, it's something you do at home before you've been anywhere or seen what things are really like. If he wants to sneer at the French for not building roads up a precipice, well, I can't stop him, but don't ask me to like him or take him seriously. I think he's an ignorant bore!'

Nigel and Margaret had not yet learned to quarrel casually, and it was possible at this point that their relationship would have suffered a significant setback, had not a shout from the direction of the car made them turn to see what was happening.

A man – they did not for the moment realise who it was – was running as though for his very life down the road towards them. They watched him in astonishment. He made straight for them, though why he should come at such speed and with such wild, contorted features, neither could imagine. Behind him the policemen waved and shouted. But it was not until the man, whom they now recognised as the driver of the car, had nearly reached them and, swerving, rushed down the hillside, that they realised he was running away. Two policemen had set off in pursuit; one drew his pistol and fired after the fugitive. But he was well ahead of them, leaping over boulders and through thorn bushes until the mist, sweeping along the hillside, swallowed him away. The police evidently thought it was useless to go after him, or perhaps they did not like the idea of walking back up the steep hillside, for they pulled up at the brink of the slope. The one with the pistol fired once, futilely, into the indifferent valley and then, turning, began to shout at Nigel.

'You let him go. Why didn't you stop him? You are his accomplice!' he yelled in bad French. He grabbed hold of Nigel's arm and hauled him back to the car.

Here, the unfortunate guide, almost weeping with terror, was already held fast by two other police.

'What's happened?' cried Margaret, running after her captive husband. 'What's happened?'

'Madam, it is a ghastly mistake! A ghastly mistake! That fellow, how was I to know he was no good? Oh, my God! What can I do? My job, my reputation –'

He was clearly in a state of near collapse, which did little to fortify the spirits of his passengers. The back seat of the car had been thrown out on the road and the explanation for his arrest was there for all to see – rifles and bren guns.

They were all bundled into the police car and transported swiftly down to Beirut.

The beauty of the scenery on that mountain road made little impression upon them, and when Beirut appeared, shining below them between the folds of two green hills, and the coast of Lebanon, misty and sunlit, stretched out in all its blue bays and gleaming peninsulas, their thoughts were too occupied with what might be done to them for them to take much notice. They remembered reports in the papers of arms smuggling into Lebanon; anyone mixed up in such activities stood the risk of being charged with subversion, for which the penalty might be anything. Of course they were not mixed up in it, but could they expect justice from a Middle East government which, if they were to believe the Iranian (furiously indignant and shouting all the way to Beirut), had such ample cause for hating the French? Not that they were French but, possibly, in the absence of any French, the English might be thought to do just as well.

They were extremely relieved when after no more than an hour in the police station, during which time they were given coffee and treated with courtesy, they were released with apologies for the inconvenience that had been caused to them. All, that is, except the guide; they heard no more of him.

'Poor chap,' said Nigel. 'You could see he had nothing to do with it. It was obviously the driver; he went for his life as soon as he saw that the game was up. But I suppose they felt they had to arrest somebody. He was rather a dear, wasn't he, Margaret?'

'Awfully nice,' she said, and smiled.

Their differences were over; the incident had had its bright side. It had brought them together again. Nigel had behaved beautifully, with such firmness and dignity. Beside him, the Iranian, chattering and expostulating angrily (and after all the police were only doing their duty), had seemed spineless, cowardly, contemptible.

Sarah was not very interested in the Thornes' experiences. She thought it to be a trivial incident. Everyone knew that arms were being smuggled into Lebanon and that Beirut was full of trouble-makers; but after all the Thornes hadn't ended up in jail and nobody had been killed, so what was all the fuss about? She had, moreover, taken a dislike to them. Margaret was hysterical and plain, and Nigel had no sense of humour. She had finished her lunch and longed to bathe and lie down; to be on her own. She wanted to review the events of the morning and looked to the time when she would be able to do so with a strange pleasure and excitement. Which was odd, because nothing very pleasant had happened to her: high explosives, blood, death – She was about to excuse herself on the grounds of weariness when Mr and Mrs Hanouche came into the room, which made it necessary to wait a little longer.

After having been introduced all round, the old couple sat down, a little apart from the others. Mr Hanouche, who was very old and rather deaf, took out his amber beads and, holding them between his knees, passed each bead slowly between his fingers. He said very little and his deafness gave him an air of remoteness so that he seemed to live in a private world with the amber beads as his only companions.

His wife was a tiny, bright-eyed woman with a quantity of thick, grey hair which she wore in a plait hanging over her shoulder. She called for her hookah, offered it to the visitors, and when it was refused, smoked it herself.

'Nadea,' she said, 'is it true that Colonel Raschid Ahmed has been murdered?'

CHAPTER 6

———

All Sarah's weariness disappeared. Colonel Raschid Ahmed. Could this be the Syrian?

'Be careful, Mrs Hanouche,' cried Nadea, 'or you'll have Sarah down on you like a ton of bricks for spreading false rumours.'

'A rumour, is it?' said Mrs Hanouche. 'I thought it probably was, coming from Cairo Radio!' The Hanouches disliked Egyptians and despised the Cairo news commentaries, but nevertheless listened to them with appalled fascination. Like most Beirutes they had become used to, and even secretly enjoyed, the atmosphere of crisis which Radio Cairo could always be counted on to provide.

'What did they say?' asked Sarah.

'They said that Colonel Ahmed had been murdered in Beirut by Lebanese government agents. It came over the eleven o'clock news.'

'There!' cried Nadea triumphantly.

'How is it,' cried Sarah, 'that Cairo Radio can broadcast this an hour before it happens?'

Mrs Hanouche was the first to grasp the import of these words. Radio Cairo had taught her the language of invective, and she employed it freely. 'So he has been killed, the murdering gangsters!' she cried. 'There's your fine hero for you, Nadea! Our poor country, poor Lebanon! These ravaging wolves are tearing us to pieces. They come into our country and murder our friends, they send agents to spy upon us! We shall all be massacred by these criminal fanatics!'

'I don't expect it was the same man,' said Nadea, her eyes flashing angrily.

'Mrs Hanouche,' said Sarah, 'who is Colonel Ahmed?'

'He is a Syrian Army officer,' cried the old lady, and went on to tell them no less vehemently what she thought of Syria.

'But what is his history?' Sarah broke in. 'What has he done? Why would he be shot?'

'Why is anyone shot? Those assassins do not want reasons for shooting people. Murder is their business. Tell them about Colonel Ahmed!' she shouted to her husband, who had sat throughout all this, staring at the carpet and caressing his beads. Everyone looked at him expectantly.

The old man's fingers dropped one bead and closed upon the next. They were not prayer beads, for he was Maronite Christian, not Moslem, and the beads had no religious meaning for him. But they were a source of comfort and an aid to meditation; the feel of the smooth, warm amber was delight to his fingers. Jolted out of his reverie he blinked his eyes, looked around at the circle of interested faces and cleared this throat. Like all Lebanese he was keenly interested in politics, and although Colonel Ahmed was not one of the most prominent figures in the Syrian politician scene, he was able to give them most of the facts known about him.

Sarah found him difficult to follow, for he spoke in bad French frequently interspersed with Arabic, and his discourse wandered into political labyrinths that were unfamiliar to her. But she gathered that Colonel Ahmed had once headed a political group in Damascus called The People's Moderate Party, which had been opposed to the present Syrian leaders and had aroused a good deal of sympathy in Lebanon because of its policy towards that country of friendship, and live-and-let-live. He was not exactly moderate as this nomenclature might suggest. No one in Syria, according to Mr Hanouche, could truthfully be called moderate, but he was less immoderate than others.

Then, six years ago, he had been arrested and thrown into jail. A series of indiscreet letters arranging for the assassinations of half a dozen prominent politicians, and even a large cheque alleged to have been discovered in the possession of a hired assassin and bearing his signature, were produced to support the charge of treason brought against him. But for some reason the whole thing had fizzled out. There were agitations. He had been popular with his fellow officers and men. It was said that the evidence had been forged and, when some of the victims named in the letters were themselves arrested for plotting against the government, Colonel Ahmed was released with a cleared name. But he disappeared from the political scene for a time and went to Europe; no more was heard of him until twelve months ago when his name cropped up during a Syrian–Lebanese crisis concerning exports into Lebanon. The Syrians, trying to blackmail the Lebanese into submission on another issue, had prohibited their normal exports into Lebanon. There had been a severe meat shortage in Beirut, which, although it had caused very little real hardship, for the Lebanese are not great meat eaters, exasperated everyone and led to anti-Muslim riots in certain predominantly Christian areas.

Colonel Ahmed had come out strongly against the policy of his own government in this affair and the Lebanese had made something of a hero of him, which exasperated the Syrians. Everyone had expected him to end up in jail again, or worse, but the opposite happened. His popularity had increased, his army commission was restored to him. The meat crisis was over by now and quickly forgotten and the colonel seemed to be getting on well with his own government, even to the extent of supporting it in some of its less extreme policies. But it was Mr Hanouche's opinion that Colonel Ahmed was simply adapting himself to a difficult situation and playing a waiting game.

'But what was he doing in Beirut?' asked Sarah. 'And why should he be shot?'

Mr Hanouche shrugged his shoulders and passed on to the next bead. He could have been shot for a hundred reasons – by a political enemy, or for personal vendetta – he belonged to an old family and almost certainly had traditional enemies, quite apart from those he had made in his own lifetime. Or he could have been shot by those of his countrymen who wanted him out of the way and preferred to do it in Beirut so that they could blame the Lebanese, or by the Lebanese themselves for reasons not yet divulged. As for why he was visiting Beirut, he could have been spying, or negotiating with the government, or simply visiting his relatives. His elder brother, Tawfik, was settled in Beirut and conducted a prosperous business in the Avenue des Francais. In any case Sarah could read about him in yesterday's *L'Orient* where – if Mr Hanouche remembered rightly – there had been a paragraph about his visit to Beirut.

Was there a copy of this paper in the house, Sarah asked, trying to keep the excitement out of her voice. A feeling of elation and anticipation took hold of her; she waited in suspense while Nadea rummaged on the divans and pulled cushions about, looking for the paper. She felt herself to be on the brink of a stupendous discovery. And it was curious, but the feeling of grief and anger she had felt for the Syrian had gone. His death was over and finished with and something new was beginning.

At last the paper was found and there, on the middle page, was a photograph. It was rather blotchy and dark and very unflattering, but there was no mistaking it. The Syrian was Colonel Raschid Ahmed.

'Colonel Raschid Ahmed, hero and martyr of the peace-loving Arab people was shot down today in cold blood in the streets of Beirut. Spies and traitors have attempted to implicate the freedom-loving Arab people in this cold-blooded murder of one of their beloved brothers. Lies are perpetrated by the Israeli stooges and their imperialist bosses. The traitors and Arab haters will be exposed for their crimes!'

Sarah leaned over and switched the radio off.

It was three o'clock, Nadea's visitors had left for their hotel; Sarah, wearing one of Nadea's housecoats (the maid was pressing her dress), was lying on Nadea's bed, while Nadea completed her packing. The blinds were drawn. It was cool and quiet in the room; every now and again the blind moved and a wedge of light appeared, white-hot, on the wall, reminding them of the sunlight outside.

In this room, on the divan in the corner, Sarah had slept during her first weeks in Beirut. It was cluttered with heavy, ugly furniture, sentimental pictures, tasteless furnishings. Wherever the eye turned it was to encounter cushions embroidered with insipid pink roses, lace doilies, china shepherdesses – when Sarah first looked on all this she had been astonished that Nadea, who always dressed with impeccable taste, seemed not to realise how hideous it all was; but ugliness can often attach itself to our affections when beauty fails to move us, and she looked around her now with a fond eye.

What a comfortably, friendly room it was; and in spite of its hotch-potch of knick-knacks, wonderfully peaceful; perhaps, because it seemed to be permanent. As long as Nadea lived there, one could be sure, nothing would be moved or changed. Some primitive instinct impelled her to cling to her few possessions, to value a bedcover or curtain that she had had since she was a child high above any that she could buy today.

If I came back in twenty years time it would be just the same, thought Sarah; the old things would stay, though there would be more ornaments and more photographs. There was one already, a new arrival, hung on the wall alongside the dressing table.

'I see you have a new boyfriend,' she remarked.

Nadea said nothing, but folded a blouse, put it in the suitcase and shrugged her shoulders. She wished she had taken the photograph down before Sarah came into the room, for with Sarah she felt it was evidence of a secret vice.

'Poor King Hussein! You're more fickle than I am! At least I stuck to Marcel for six months. Why don't you get married and stop worshipping public men?'

'Why don't you get married yourself?' retorted Nadea, looking up under low, scowling brows.

'I will – to the next one.'

'Well I won't – ever! How can you waste your life chasing around with worthless men like Marcel? There's something horribly servile about you, Sarah. You seem actually to enjoy shelving all your ability so that some man can have the satisfaction of shoving you around.'

'That's all I've talent for,' said Sarah smiling. She stretched her legs and was sharply aware of her own body – sleek and warm, and free again, uncommitted, expectant, recharging its energies. Nadea's right, she thought, I'm undiscriminating, wasteful of my affections; well, I've finished with the Marcels of this world. Next time I meet an attractive man I shall bring a little intelligence to bear upon him. But in the very moment of making this resolve her thoughts had drifted away from it, borne, involuntarily, by a perverse and romantic streak in her nature.

'And by the look on your face,' said Nadea, 'I can see you've someone else in mind already. Really Sarah, here are we Jordanian women struggling for some kind of status, and people like you –' She broke off and ended, expostulating violently, 'Marriage! There's too much I want to do with my life.'

She spoke sincerely. She had no intention of marrying, although many men would have been glad to marry her. She was a patriot. She was not interested in men, only in heroes; she had never felt love for a man, only an impersonal adoration. Her first hero had been Glub Pasha, the English soldier and leader of the Arab Legion; then the young monarch of Jordan, King Hussein, had won her devotion. And now a picture of the Egyptian dictator, Gamel Abdul Nasser, hung from her wall.

Every time she listened to his broadcast speeches from Cairo her heart beat with anger and pride, as it was intended that it should – and her reason was submerged. In her more clear-sighted moments she knew this, but the charm of her new hero held her captive; he had brought drama and excitement into her life that she could not now bear to give up. He had attacked her insidiously where she was most vulnerable, demanding a new dedication to his cause where she was most eager to give it – in her hatred of Israel. Her brother had been killed by the Jews, her friends and family had lost their land, her country had suffered humiliation and misery, and the Egyptian dictator asked her only to hate; not to control her passions, to think, to be just, to be constructive, only to hate. Such an appeal was irresistible.

'You don't understand,' she cried. 'You're not an Arab! He's given us Arabs something. He's made us feel proud.'

'What do you mean, "us Arabs"? You Jordanians are Arabs, the Egyptians aren't. How did they get on this Arab bandwagon, anyway? They're only making capital out of your misfortunes.'

Nadea was silent. Her position was hard to defend because in her heart she despised the Egyptians as she despised the Lebanese, who were a soft, money-loving people, corrupted by a long association with the French; and the Egyptians were what they had always been, a mongrel lot – Negro, Berber, Somali, Nubian – with none of the Bedouins' toughness, generosity and courage.

'Now if you and the Israelis would only get tougher,' said Sarah, yawning.

'We'll never get together! We'd rather die first!'

'And in the meantime you play into the hands of any bandit who likes to shout out, "Down with the Jews!" One of these days, Nadea, one of your self–appointed champions of Arab nationalism will go too far and destroy the lot of you.'

'Perhaps we don't care,' cried Nadea excitedly. 'If we go up in smoke you'll go up with us. We shall have had our day. That's something you damn British never allowed us.'

'Well, if all you want is to blow up the world, any fool can do that.'

'That's not the point! Suppose we are impossible. Why don't you leave us alone to make our own mess?'

'If we'd left you alone you'd still be being shoved around by those adorable Turks. You shout and scream at us and conveniently forget all that.'

'What if we do shout and scream?' shouted Nadea. 'That's our way of doing things. We like shouting. We know what we want and don't want you damn efficient snooty British telling us how we should live our lives!'

'Darling, don't you know the British are a dead duck? You're so busy kicking that poor old corpse around you don't even know you're being fattened up for someone else's stew.'

'Well, the Americans then, they're worse. They don't even understand us, and they expect us to be grateful when they do things for us that suit themselves.'

'All right, I admit everything. We're all impossible except you angelic Arabs, and don't delude yourselves into thinking we're interested in you. I only wish all your oil would dry up and we could clear out and leave you to stew in your own juice.'

Suddenly Nadea laughed. 'Sarah, I'm so glad you're back!' She shut the lid of her suitcase and fastened the catches. 'Now while I'm gone, you won't go back to Marcel?'

Sarah smiled at her lovingly. She put out her hand and their fingers touched. 'Nadea, when I make up my mind, do I ever?'

'No, but you're such a fool about men. I only wish I could get you interested in my village work. Sarah, why do you have to be so frivolous?'

'I don't believe in charity – your sort, I mean.'

'You say that. You don't mean it. You're just selfish and lazy.' She leaned over and kissed Sarah's cheek, her dark hair swinging forward over her face. 'I've told Alexa to get your suitcase from Dobbies. There's money in your bag. Now, must rush.'

When Nadea had gone Sarah felt lonely. It was not that she was troubled about the future. After all, Nadea had left her with plenty of money, and she was only going to Amman for four days. The feeling was more complicated than that. She had known before this restlessness and sense of loss when she had been separated from someone she had loved. Nothing was urgent or important. Time had stopped for her, although it was still going on for others.

She lay, unable to sleep, although she was tired, distracted by the sounds coming from the street outside. She realised after a moment that she was listening to these sounds – the honking of horns, the jabber of a badly tuned wireless set, the cry of street vendors – and identifying them, as though she were expecting one of them to contain a special message for her. She was waiting for something to happen; perhaps she was even expecting the door to open and someone to come into the room.

But who? Could it be Marcel? She considered the possibility carefully. But no, she felt quite different towards Marcel; she did not want to see him again and was not even curious to know how he had reacted to her departure. The past few hours had made it impossible for her to love Marcel or anyone like him again. Yet the feeling of being in love remained – the sadness, loneliness and exhilaration.

At length, she got up and picked up the paper containing the Syrian's photograph. For the third time she read the caption beneath it. 'Colonel Raschid Ahmed, who arrived in Beirut today as the Syrian government delegate in the forthcoming negotiations for a revision of the trade agreement with Lebanon.'

It was a bad photograph. It made him look thick-necked, and square-jawed, when he had been so handsome. In spite of the pink car and the terrible tie . . .

Like a beautiful thoroughbred horse, thought Sarah, dressed up for a circus.

And then she began to feel drowsy and, putting the paper down on the bed beside her, turned over contentedly and went to sleep.

CHAPTER 7

In the meantime, Beirut, almost without realising what had happened, was in the midst of another crisis.

Disturbances in the French suk that morning had spread to the Muslim quarter. Most shopkeepers had put up their shutters and retired, like crabs into their holes, to await the calming of political passions; and those who had not immediately shut up shop had been forced under the threat of dire consequences to follow suit. There were rumours of a general strike, and Ras Beirut was full of people getting in supplies for a week or so. Coffee quickly became unobtainable and the price of sugar went up by twenty-five piastres a kilo.

No-one knew exactly what the crisis was about, though it was clear that Syrian-Lebanese relations had suddenly drastically deteriorated, just at a time when it had seemed that they might be improving. The answer to it all – though what it was no one could agree – was to be found in the murder of Colonel Raschid Ahmed (that the murdered man was Colonel Ahmed was by now generally accepted), although, strangely enough, there had been no mention of his assassination in the news broadcast from Beirut.

Radio Cairo on the other hand had hardly stopped talking about him since their eleven o'clock news that morning. They took the line that Colonel Ahmed had been the victim of a plot, hatched up by the Americans and executed by the Lebanese Liberals (the party then in power), to thwart Syria in her efforts to live in peace and friendship with Lebanon. The disturbances in the suks, the new commentator declared, were the angry protests of the loyal Lebanese people, who were stricken with grief and rage over this blow dealt at the great cause of Arab unity.

Supporters of the Lebanese government naturally took the opposite view, that the Egyptians and the Syrians had murdered Colonel Ahmed to provide themselves with an excuse for a renewed campaign against Lebanon and that the trouble in the suks had been caused by professional Syrian agitators and discontented Palestinian refugees. But as the government itself was strangely silent about the incident, a good many people accepted Radio Cairo's explanation, particularly after hearing it three or four times, for the people of the Middle East are most easily persuaded by constant repetition. A few thoughtful ones pointed out the weak places in Cairo Radio's argument – the fact, for instance, that protests against the murder of Colonel Ahmed, if such they had been, had apparently preceded his death, and that Radio Cairo had announced the assassination over an hour before it had happened. But these small slips, although they might have carried weight elsewhere, did not matter much in the present situation. Most people by this time were either persuaded and did not want to look for the truth, or were too confused to recognise it. And everyone had forgotten the sequence in which events had happened, except those who particularly wanted to remember them.

To add to the confusion the events of the morning had produced a whole harvest of rumours. There were the usual alarms that broke out at every crisis. Bombs had been thrown at the British Embassy; a cache of arms, enough to equip the entire Muslim population of Lebanon, had been found in the Egyptian Embassy; Russian planes had landed at the Damascus airport; the American fleet was steaming up the Mediterranean. Nobody took these rumours very seriously – they had been heard too often before – but there were others whose freshness and originality commanded more respect.

It was said, for instance, that the murdered man was not Colonel Raschid Ahmed at all, but a certain Yusef Kassim of the Syrian military police, who had fled to Lebanon for asylum and, knowing that hired assassins had followed him, had staged his own death and been whisked away into hiding by friends who were now engaged in smuggling him out of the country. Another report had reached Beirut that Syrian spies disguised as tourists had been caught by the police at Sofar on the Damascus road. It was takenfor granted that terrorism should break out in such habitual trouble spots as Tripoli and Tyre, but people were shocked to hear that in the quiet little Maronite village of Dhat Rhas a bomb had been exploded in a butcher's shop, killing, fortunately, only a cow.

Reports of violence and the expectation of more to come, had their usual effect upon the mood of Beirut. Sullen, hot-eyed youths hung about on corners glaring at anyone passing by who happened to have blonde hair; and there was a noticeable increase in the belligerence of taxi drivers who, if they had not already done so, stuck pictures of their patrons – Colonel Nasser or the Virgin Mary – on their windscreens and drove about noisily trying to force their opponents off the road.

It must not be supposed, however, that people stayed shut up in their homes, depressed or panic-stricken. The Lebanese, as has already been said, take their fears lightly, and there were many who looked upon the events of the day as providing a good excuse for an afternoon's outing. Sightseers in large cars streamed into Ras Beirut to see if anything else was afoot and to inspect the bullet marks on the pavement of Rue Zahle. The Corniche in front of the American University and on the cliffs above Pigeon Rock was crowded with people on foot and cruising backwards and forwards in their cars, enjoying the sunshine and the spectacle of other people being stopped and searched by the police.

The swimming clubs were crowded as usual, and here nobody even thought about Syria or Colonel Ahmed. Swimmers, paddling about in the tideless blue water, could look back to land and see their city spread out along the coast in all its happy security. Behind it the mountains, dim purple and scarred with snow, rose so precipitously they seemed to crowd the white buildings down to the very brink of the water. It is impossible, in Beirut, to forget the mountains; they lend solemnity to a city tending to be feckless, imposing from afar a beauty that disintegrates in the untidy streets. Indeed, of Beirut itself little enough is required, for the mountains lend its splendour just as the sea, lapping at the golden corrugated cliffs, lends it gaiety. And they have another function, sensed dimly and comforting to those Lebanese swimmers splashing about in blue pools or lying exhausted with sunshine amongst a crop of coloured umbrellas – for centuries they have isolated this coastline and guarded its ancient cities. No breath of the desert touches the fertile plane. The snows stand between.

Today, of course, they could no longer look for protection to rivers and mountain ranges, for men have learned subtler ways of infiltration. But the mind is slow to give up its ancient securities, and the Lebanese, living as they do under the shadow of that great rock which in the past required only a handful of soldiers and a fortress here and there to keep invading armies back, felt vaguely that they could depend upon it still, and accepted their troubles with nonchalance, almost, one might say, savouring them as one of the varied flavours of the idle afternoon.

Sarah slept for an hour. At four–thirty she awoke, dressed, and went out. She had no particular destination in mind and walked idly and inattentively down the street without noticing a car parked opposite the Hanouches' house, or the watchful, earnest face that stared at her over the wheel.

The scene at first glance looked pretty much as usual. In the flats opposite a fat man in brown and white striped pyjamas stood on his balcony eating loquats and spitting the shiny brown seeds onto the road. Young girls wearing cotton skirts that billowed out around their hips like huge, inverted, full-petalled flowers, tripped off for the Corniche, swimming suits and rolled up towels tucked under their arms. Every shop and flat, it seemed, had its wireless set going at full blast, but this again was much as usual, and Sarah, who did not understand Arabic, was not to know what inflammatory stuff was being churned out into the clear air around her.

She came to Rue Zahle and looked up it with a queer, irrational eagerness.

There was the pavement where they had stood in the morning sunshine; now the long, still shadows of the afternoon lay across it. There was the house that he had never entered, the high wall, the pomegranate trees with their waxy red flowers. Whom had he been going to meet? A friend and colleague, he had said. The house was closed, the blue shutters fastened.

That morning, apart from the old man in the flannel nightgown and the children playing on the heap of rubble, they had been alone in the Rue Zahle. Now cars, disregarding the one way street sign, drove back and forth along it. One of the beggar children usually to be seen hanging about the gates of the American University – a black-eyed, red-headed brat with long beads dangling down over her ragged dress – was acting as guide to a group of youths who had come, presumably, to inspect the blood stains.

Sarah came to the travel agency. The door was shut and there was a notice hanging inside saying, 'Closed for today. Enquire No. 12, 4th Floor, Flat 24.' No. 12 was an apartment building next door to the agency.

Sarah did not look again up Rue Zahle. One look had been enough. It had given her a queer, unpleasant shock, as though someone had confirmed bad news which, so far, she had discounted. Instead she looked at the large mounted photographs in the travel agency window, the six famous columns of Baalbek: the court-yard of the palace at Beit ed Din, the source of Nahr Ibrahim, the Adonis River, at Akfar in the mountains.

Sarah had naturally been to Baalbek and Beit ed Din several times; these were two of the celebrated sights of Lebanon. She had also been, once, with Marcel, only a month ago, to the source of the Adonis, had climbed about among the fallen stones of Aphrodite's temple, and peered into the grotto where pictures of the Virgin Mary now made claim for Christianity on the ancient holy places of the pagan goddess.

It had been early spring. Pale primroses and cyclamen with rose-tipped petals and leaves mottled like the skins of green snakes grew in thick clusters from the rocks and nodded under the splash of the ice-cold torrents. Marcel, Sarah remembered, bored by the abundance of scenery – nothing but rock and cloud and gushing waters, not a café in sight nor the prospect of a glass of arak for hours – had wanted to leave almost the moment they got there and had sat on a rock sulking while Sarah climbed about with the guide. This old Akura peasant had leapt from rock to rock, supporting Sarah with firm, strong hands. His hair and upturned moustaches were white, his face youthful and brown, and he had had the tiniest feet shod with rubber galoshes; mountain feet, Sarah supposed, designed like the feet of a goat for scampering over boulders and up precipices.

He had shown her the source of the sacred river – a white torrent gushing out from the gaping cliff. He had pointed out columns of rosy Egyptian granite lying amongst the temple ruins and had ordered her to kneel by the grotto and pray to the Lady of the Place, a command with which she had complied, sharing her prayer impartially between the Virgin Mary and the Goddess of Love and asking of the one that which it did not seem politic to ask of the other. He had then pointed up to the cloud-draped cliffs and by means of a little stilted and mispronounced French let it be known that over a pass the Roman road built by the Emperor Domitian had led pilgrims down to the other side of the mountain, where they had completed the rites of Aphrodite at another temple by a lake hidden in the low hills overlooking the Beka'a.

That spring day – the old guide with his narrow light feet, the seething waters of the sacred river – came back to her vividly as she walked on away from the travel agency. She dwelt on it, trying to remember every detail of what had happened and what had been said, for she had suddenly recalled that it had been on that day, at that spot, that she had first heard of Ain Houssaine.

Wondering what had impelled Colonel Ahmed to pronounce that name with his dying breath, she turned the corner into Avenue Bliss and collided with two youths standing in the middle of the pavement. They made no attempt to get out of her way but stared at her insolently, and one of them made the smallest, aggressive movement, as though to strike her.

So we're in for another crisis, she thought with surprise and dodged past the young men into a bookshop.

There were a lot of people in the shop, but nobody seemed to be buying anything; they were all standing about talking in low, earnest voices. Sarah went across to the Middle East section and looked through the shelves for a guide book to Lebanon. She found one at length and opened it at the index.

More people entered the shop. An American child heavily armed with two large toy pistols rushed about holding people up, but nobody took any notice. The watchwords of crisis – *Egypt, Suez, Jews, Muslims, refugees* – whispered about the shop like the first soft gusts of wind heralding a storm.

'The Israelis are a fact,' someone behind Sarah was saying. 'They forced their way in; they had the advantage of desperation. We can't shut our eyes to them; we must accept them.'

'You can't count on the Americans. Look how they let the British down.'

'Of course if they cut the pipelines –'

'Do you think there would be an opening in Australia for a good Lebanese restaurant?' a tall, sad–eyed youth inquired of a freckled girl.

Sarah turned a page and began to read.

'It is not easy to get to Ain Houssaine. The village is situated on the eastern flank of Mount Lebanon in a landlocked valley, some twenty miles north-west of Baalbek. An unmade road leads into the valley from the Beka'a.

'A more picturesque and romantic way, taking some five hours, is to walk over Emperor Domitian's road from Akura on the other side of Mount Lebanon, as did the Adonis pilgrims of 2000 years ago. The devotees, after performing spring-time fertility rites at the Akfa temple, crossed the mountain by this road and threw themselves into Lake Houssaine for ceremonial purification –'

'Madame Gautier! Madame Gautier!'

Sarah closed the book and turned. The short, fat man with curly black hair who was hurrying across the shop towards her was Professor Adib, her former French teacher. She had stopped her lessons a month before and was not pleased to see him again. Under the pretext of French custom he had kissed her hand more often than necessary and had delighting in teaching her words which, in Sarah's opinion, were easily looked up in the dictionary.

'Do you think there's going to be any trouble?' she asked in French, backing behind a pile of books. Professor Adib's eyes sparkled with excitement. His instinct was to predict the worst, but his duty, as he saw it, was to shield a lady from alarm. 'No, I think not, Madame. A strike tomorrow probably. There has been a quantity of inflammatory pamphlets distributed around the suks. But you need not be nervous. In Dhat Rhas you are among friends. The bit of trouble they had there was soon dealt with.'

'Trouble in Dhat Rhas?'

'You haven't heard? They have been throwing bombs in

a butcher's shop . . . quite an outbreak of terrorism . . . but it's all well in hand. In Lebanon we look after our guests, Madame, particularly' – a hand on his heart – 'when they are so charming, so intelligent.'

'But Beirut' – Sarah interrupted these gallantries with the first thing that came into her head – 'there's a nasty atmosphere. Haven't you seen –'

'*Vu, madame! Vu, vu, vu! Faites donc attention a cette voyelle!*'

'*Vu*,' repeated Sarah, submissively.

'Very good. But you must be careful. You are getting careless. As for Beirut – these agitators . . .' He dismissed them with a disdainful flip of his fingers. 'Syrians, Jordanians. We Lebanese can look after ourselves. Now they are throwing the Lebanese out of Cairo – you wait and see – they can't live without us. We are a hundred years ahead of Egypt.'

'Yes, but there are more of them.'

He lowered his voice and leaned closer to her. Sarah backed away. 'Have you been to Egypt? I have. It is impoverished, bankrupt; the peasants half dead, the administrators corrupt. They thought they could get rid of corruption by throwing out their king. *Pouf!* Corruption is in the marrow of their bones.'

'They've raised a flag and fashioned a cause,' said Sarah, regarding with him distaste. 'What cause have you got except trade and easy living?'

'A cause!' Professor Adib was contemptuous. 'Flags go up and down all over the Middle East, Madame. A cause is born in the morning and dead at night. This is all emptiness – full of air like a great balloon. Prick it and it bursts – *pouf!* When people have nothing to say they curse. What is this cause you are talking about? Just a string of curses.' But he looked depressed nevertheless.

'Well, it seems to me you can't dismiss all this quite so lightly. After all there are quite a few people in this country who are thoroughly fed up.'

'*Pay–yee! Pay–yee, Madame! C'est une faux tres grave. Faites attention! Alors . . . repetez encore une fois.*'

'*Pay–yee,*' said Sarah, mastering her fury.

'*C'est ca.* Do not distress yourself, Madame. This whole thing will fizzle out. The Egyptians are trying to whip up feeling over the murder of Colonel Ahmed, but you see our government has had long experience of these tactics. They are waiting and saying nothing, and when the time comes they will play their winning card.'

'What card?' asked Sarah, and this time she did not mind leaning closer to catch his reply.

He lowered his voice and cast a quick glance around him. 'They will produce Colonel Ahmed,' he whispered.

'*But he's dead!*'

Professor Adib smiled a benign, insinuating smile and half closed his eyes. 'Do you think so, Madam? I think not.'

'How do you know? What do you know?'

But his reply was disappointingly obtuse. 'Forty years of living in Beirut, watching the wind blow and that . . . You are a foreigner, Madame, you cannot expect to understand. What's more you live on an island. We Lebanese are masters in the art of survival. We are Europeans, don't forget, we live on Europe's edge with Asia all around us. Asia has forced us into intrigue. Now we can beat them at their own game.'

'That means nothing. You're only guessing.'

'Listen, Madame, the government has said nothing. They are silent. There was no mention of this murder on the Beirut news; this evening the papers are censored. Accusations have been brought against them; they do not defend themselves. Why? Because they do not need to. This silence would be dangerous to them if they did not have a card up their sleeve.'

It's just an idea he has; he doesn't know anything, thought Sarah. But he had sown a hope in her mind that would not be stifled. It sprang up and prospered.

After Professor Adib had gone Sarah left the shop and stood for a moment on the pavement wondering what to do. Outside the gate of the American University students stood about talking excitedly and small boys had abandoned their usual occupations of selling postcards and chewing gum to throw stones at passing cars. The scene was further enlivened by a traffic jam – a car, trying to turn round in the middle of the narrow street had got stuck in front of a tram and there was no room to pass on either side, for the road had been torn up down one side of the tramline and was in the process of being repaired, as usual.

Sarah crossed the road, passed through the university and entered the quiet shade of the garden. She used to walk here often in the evenings when she had been living in Rhas Beirut, and made her way now to a seat that commanded a view down the terraced slope to the sea beyond.

There were few people about. Two suntanned girls played tennis on the court below and students strolled along the paths between the lawns. Sarah was hardly conscious of them. They seemed effaced by trees and flowers, and she could barely hear the thud of tennis balls for the shriek of cicadas.

The sun, falling westward over the sea, struck the face of the hill, flushing the warm stone of the university buildings. Oleanders planted on the terraced hillside foamed in extravagant pink clouds at Sarah's feet, and hibiscus blooms, nodding against the sky, filtered the light like stained-glass through their crimson petals.

Sarah sat alone on the garden seat. Her mood had changed at the moment of entering the garden. She was suddenly happy and, looking about her at the bronze red pine needles scattered on the pathways and the eucalyptus blossom hanging in hazy clusters, felt such joy she might never have seen such loveliness before. A cricket began singing on a shrill, incessant note, right under her foot. She listened and felt she could feel the earth vibrating. She stamped her foot and silenced not only the cricket, but the cicadas in the pine trees over her head, which at once fell utterly still.

The quiet sounded strange, a gap had opened in the afternoon. Then in the intense silence she heard a footstep. She turned to look back over her shoulder.

A man stood directly behind her, looking at her with an expression of grave attention. She almost cried out.

He came a step nearer and nervously licked his lips. 'I want to speak with you. Don't be afraid,' he said in a low voice.

He was a short, rather stocky man, around fifty. Good-looking in his youth, probably, but now he had lost most of his hair and his features had become square and heavy; one would guess that rich food and heavy living had coarsened him. But his nose, which was narrow and aquiline, and his eyes, which had so startled her, leant distinction to his face.

He gave a quick, apprehensive glance behind him and slipped into the seat at Sarah's side. She could not imagine what he wanted with her, and after that first, devastating flash of recognition, had realised that he was a stranger, but it did not occur to her to move away.

'Please understand,' he said, speaking in a low agitated voice, 'I have nothing to do with this. I wouldn't be here at all if it weren't – well we won't go into that . . . But I don't want you to think that you can make any demands on me. I'm a respectable citizen leading a decent honest life, and all I'm interested in is keeping my family in reasonable comfort and security. This kind of thing is extremely dangerous to me and I undertake it only with the greatest reluctance. Do you understand?'

'I don't understand at all.'

'I'm explaining to you that you must not assume you have an ally in me. I am neutral, Mademoiselle. He should never have asked this of me; he knows how I feel. I am a family man with children and responsibilities. And being Syrian I have to be careful. They think we are trouble makers, and they have good reason. I have to move with great caution, my reputation is precious to me –'

He broke off when Sarah turned and stared at him earnestly. 'Please, don't look at me, Mademoiselle! Look straight ahead!'

'Why? Is someone watching us?'

'How can I tell? You are known to the police. And to others. You were with him. I had to choose between a meeting place like this and going openly to your house, which would have been even more incautious. So I followed you here. As it is, heaven knows, there may be unpleasant repercussions for me.'

Sarah sat staring straight ahead into the oleanders, as he had commanded. A bird with a curved bill sipped honey from their flowers. How small it was, how exquisite, its bill like a thin metal probe, its bright eye . . . For a moment, looking at the bird, and tense with happiness, she forgot what they were talking about. 'Who are you?' she murmured.

'That is irrelevant. Have I been talking for nothing?' he broke out angrily. 'I've told you, I was forced into this against my will, even tricked, you might say. The whole point is, Mademoiselle – who are you?'

She could not resist turning again to look at him. 'Don't you know?'

He too seemed to be losing his cautiousness for his eyes rested for a moment on her face. The expression in them was curious; he seemed almost afraid of her and surprised and admiring, as though she were dangerous, but at the same time admirable. 'You must tell me.'

Sarah, staring into his eyes, felt a rush of emotion. They were so alike. He must be an elder brother, she thought.

'Sarah Lane.'

'And your address?'

'5 Rue Jeanne d'Arc.'

He nodded. 'Can you prove this? An identity card, a passport?'

'No, I can't, you see I lost my passport this morning. 'There was –'

'Yes, yes, I know. It is difficult. I shall have to trust you.' He seemed to relax slightly. He leant back in the seat and crossed his legs, though he still did not look at her. 'You probably think me over-cautious, Mademoiselle, and I don't mean to be ungracious, of course. When Raschid rang me this morning I thought – you will excuse me if I confess what I thought but after all it was a natural supposition – there is some explanation. But what would you have thought under the circumstances? He put it in such a way that I naturally supposed it to be a personal matter. To put it brutally, the termination of a relationship. Consolation, as it were. I perfectly understood that he would want someone else to act for him – no scenes, no tears. Most young women would be only too happy, but their pride nevertheless demands that they indulge in unpleasant recriminations. Well, now, it was no more than an hour later when I heard of this dastardly attack that I realised I had been quite mistaken. But Raschid wanted me to be mistaken, that is the point, and this makes me angry. But I promised and I must keep my word or he'll never forgive me. There, there it is.'

'But I don't –'

'I don't want to know what you're doing. I don't want to know anything about it.'

Sarah looked down at the bundle of money that he had put in her hands. She had never held so much money in her life before. While he had been speaking tears had surged into her eyes; now they ran down her cheeks. 'But I can't take this,' she sobbed, 'I've done nothing!'

'I don't known anything about that,' replied the man at her side, looking at her curiously, as though her distress puzzled him.

'It was only thirty pounds – what I lost in my bag – and even if you count in the air ticket. I did nothing at all. I just sat for an hour.'

He did not move; he sat silent. Sarah turned to look at him and found him staring at her with an expression of scorn and loathing. She was so startled her tears dried.

'Ah! Mademoiselle!' he said with bitter reproach. 'When a man is helpless and can only trust in his friends –'

'But he's dead!'

Their eyes met. Sarah's blue and imploring, his angry and hard. 'So that is the line you are going to adopt,' he said slowly. 'I understand.' He got up and without another word to her began to walk hurriedly away.

'What must I do?' she called after him.

He did not reply, but she knew he had heard her for he shook his head quickly back and forth, throwing her question, her plea, away from him. A moment later he had disappeared around a bend in the pathway.

She sat, staring down at the notes in her hand, and then opened her handbag to put them inside.

Sarah had not until that moment examined the interior of the bag that Colonel Ahmed had given her that morning. She had imagined it was empty; there had been no point in opening it. The hundred Lebanese pounds that Nadea had lent her Nadea herself had put into the bag. So it was now, for the first time, that she saw the two letters.

The first was addressed to Mr Emile Khalife, Chakra. The second to herself. She opened hers and began to read.

As the afternoon drew on and the sun, sinking lower, struck fully on the western face of Beirut, the pink, gold and white of the thickly-clustered buildings fused together into one white-hot glare. On top of the cliffs above Pigeon Rock the windows of apartment houses blazed into sheets of gold, and every now and again a light flashed like a signal out to sea, as a car on the road that mounted the cliffs caught the sun on its windscreen.

The city seemed to lose itself in this shower of light, and the mountains behind and the sea drew closer upon each other. The tall, square buildings close to the sea's edge looked like mere extensions of the salt-white cliffs, and on the mountain slopes villages and towns hung in the dark-green felt of pine forests.

As the sun declined further, people drove out of Beirut instinctively seeking something not to be found within the crowded streets, something they encountered on the tops of cliffs watching the fishing boats return to shore, or out on the empty red sand-dunes, which, disordered and desolate under the noonday sun, now seemed mysterious and beautiful.

Sarah, possessed by a restlessness and impatience that was almost insupportable, left the university and, calling a taxi, told the driver to take her to the airport and back.

'Slowly! Slowly!' she cried, as they careered with screaming tyres around the Corniche and out into the open road by the swimming clubs.

The dunes burned copper red in the declining sun. Long shadows lay flung across the sand, printing as inky patches every footprint threading the ridges. Clumps of umbrella pines stood intensely still and gathered into themselves, woven into one mass by the closeness of their growth and the unity of their shadows. On the outskirts of these little forests, nomads had pitched their tents and here and there a donkey with a hairy foal trotting behind it wandered over the sand hills. And jockeys from the racecourse, who had been exercising their horses, were now riding home.

Sarah, looking out of the taxi window, saw a grey stallion dancing with arched neck under the hand of its rider. The sand spouting up hung like fire around its hoofs. It reminded her of Colonel Ahmed. Leaning forward she told the taxi driver to take her back to Rue Jeanne d'Arc.

Here, as darkness fell, she sat waiting on the verandah amongst Nadea's ferns and climbing plants.

The cheek of it! she thought. Telling his brother that he was buying me off...

But the big gloomy clock in the hall struck seven, eight, nine, and he did not come. The long suspense, the clinging to a vain hope, had exhausted her. If I wait any longer, she told herself, I shall go off my head. I must do something. I must get help.

She did not in fact want help so much as to tell someone what had happened; to win from someone else confirmation of what she wanted to believe, for faith is strengthened mightily if another shares it.

If only Nadea were here, she thought. But Nadea was in Amman and most of Sarah's other acquaintances had been Marcel's friends and were unsuited to the role of confidant and protector. Moreover, she was determined against making any move that might connect her again, however tenuously, with Marcel.

At 9:30 she left the house and turned down Rue Jeanne d'Arc in the direction of the travel agency.

CHAPTER 8

Alan Crawe lived in a fourth-floor apartment next to the travel agency. The building was designed around an open courtyard that served as a place to hang washing and a dump for rubbish and which trapped and magnified the noise of wireless sets, parties and family disputes coming from the rooms around it.

Alan had become accustomed to the noise, which in any case in Ras Beirut was inescapable, and had grown attached to his neighbours, whose lusty domestic life was daily and nightly exposed for his edification. Moreover, he had a view, which in Beirut was hard to acquire, and with the rate that buildings were shooting up, harder still to keep. By some happy chance his apartment was so situated that from his bedroom window he could look out north eastwards through the narrow spaces between buildings and could actually see the mountains; when darkness fell the lights of Aley and Broumana hung above his head like a great crowd of twinkling, intimate stars swarming too close to earth; and from his front balcony he could look across the road over unfinished roof tops to a strip of blue sea.

When Sarah rang his doorbell that evening, Alan was talking to his partner, Ishmael Qazzaz. They had spent an afternoon terrifying for the one and exasperating for the other – Ishmael in jail, Alan trying to get him out – and were now discussing their experience over a bottle of arak.

It was the second time that Alan had prised Ishmael from the clutches of the Lebanese police. The first of these occasions had marked the beginning of, and put its stamp upon, their friendship.

It had happened three years before in a narrow one-way street not far from the French suk. Ishmael, disregarding the one-way sign, had turned his car up the street and, finding his progress blocked by a taxi which was coming down it, had been forced to stop. He was clearly in the wrong but, feeling himself unable to give way to a mere taxi driver (and a rude one at that), had refused to back his car. The taxi driver abused him, and a crowd of onlookers collected, listened to the case for both sides and split into factions, some taking the part of the taxi driver, others – the admirers of pride and intransigence – supporting Ishmael. In the meantime a long line of traffic was piling up behind the taxi and Alan, whose taxi it was, got out and tried to reason with Ishmael.

Ishmael liked Alan on sight and thanked him for his courteous behaviour but, by now, nothing less than his honour was at stake and, to prove that he was willing to stick to his guns all day if necessary, he unfolded his daily paper and began to read it – albeit inattentively. This infuriated the taxi driver and those among the crowd who had taken his side. People shouted, horns honked. Moderates pleaded with both parties and suggested a compromise.

Could not both cars back at the same time at a given signal? But this was no longer possible for, traffic having piled up behind the taxi, there was now no place for it to back into.

At this point the police arrived and joined in the argument. They sympathised with Ishmael's point of view and, to begin with, reasoned with him gently. He had no right, they pointed out, to be going up a down street in the first place. Most people had overlooked this point and a few onlookers changed sides, attacking Ishmael with all the virulence of converts. A brawl broke out and several people were arrested, including Ishmael.

After a few hours in jail he was set free and, on discovering that it was Alan who had engineered his release, all but flung his arms around his rescuer's neck. This gesture of friendship from a stranger, and one, moreover, who by nature of the fact that he had been occupying the offending taxi must have felt himself on the opposing side, seemed to him to be extraordinarily touching and beautiful. And so was born one of those cleaving, illogical, oriental attachments which come about, as often as not, from a mere chance circumstance, but are none the less fervent for that.

The outcome of this incident was that Alan resigned from his job in London (he had been on holiday) and joined Ishmael in the travel agency which, under Ishmael's direction, had been running unnoticeably into bankruptcy. All his friends told him he was mad but he was young enough, at thirty-three, to face the prospect of losing all his money without grave alarm. And on the whole they had done very well.

The agency, now renamed Anglo-Lebanese Travels Ltd, revived considerably. There were the usual difficulties of working in a country where one is not a national, but when these were overcome business went ahead. By luck they secured a government contract and in a rush of optimism bought two new cars. So far, most of their business had come from airline bookings; now they started doing tours in Lebanon and between Beirut and Damascus. These were a great success, and they discussed the possibility of opening a London branch.

The two men made a good team. Alan had a flair for business; he put the chaotic accounts in order and built up a smoothly running organisation, leaving Ishmael and Ishmael's sister Georgette to deal with their clients, for whom, he quickly found, he had little liking.

The excursions within Lebanon had been Alan's idea. Being well read in Middle East history and interested in archaeology, he had planned them as lecture tours and hoped that they would be both enjoyable and instructive. But they had proved quite intolerable. He had no patience with his hapless charges – he derided the informed and insulted the ignorant. Finally he gave up after a particularly trying afternoon spent at Sidon with a party of Australians whose profound ignorance goaded him into terminating the tour an hour before the appointed time on the grounds that 'the whole thing was utterly wasted on them'.

From that day Ishmael replaced him as the guide, to the relief of all concerned. Everyone liked the young Jordanian; his pleasant appearance and friendly manner inspired, if not confidence, at any rate a certain tolerant affection. Though inefficient, he was tirelessly helpful, and customers, remembering his charm and forgiving his mistakes, usually returned. Ishmael was in his element, for he loved company and going on picnics, which was what these once scholarly excursions had now become. And Alan was happy behind his desk working on his accounts, making new plans and keeping a watchful eye on his partner.

It must be admitted that the two were not without their differences. Ishmael, although he had spent six years in London, was an Arab and had his own way of doing things. There was something about Alan's methodical ways, his scrupulous respect for the law, his efficiency – even the neatness of his account books and the symmetrical arrangement of files upon his desk – that irked Ishmael and aroused in him all manner of perverse desires. He was like a child who, when confronted with a still, clear pool of water, cannot resist plunging in its hand and stirring up the mud on the bottom. Alan made rules – Ishmael broke them. If an opportunity presented itself to bribe a frontier policemen, to cheat the customs, to put something over the airways companies – even if it brought him no profit – he clutched it eagerly. He could not bear not to be almost in trouble.

So it was that Anglo-Lebanese Travels Ltd operated

rather like a Middle Eastern state under mandate to a western power – with Alan doggedly building up an organisation of the most scrupulous legality and orderliness whose foundations Ishmael was quietly undermining. Such as well-proportioned and solidly-built edifice was a challenge to his native ingenuity.

Yet this is not the full picture, for Ishmael was revolting against tyranny. Alan, though recognising his qualities – his good humour, his generosity, his openness of heart – was impatient with his faults and tended to brush aside his opinions as unworthy of notice. Ishmael's devotion to his partner had not diminished. He felt irrevocably indebted to him and was not resentful of this debt as it was a source of intense happiness to him; but he also sensed, with alarm, a lessening, a sinking as it were, of his own identity and was constantly feeling about him for some means of reasserting it. He possessed, as the circumstances of his meeting with Alan will have illustrated, a great deal of pride, towards which the young Englishman was not always sufficiently tender. It was a pride, moreover, that had received some hard knocks over the past few years. For Ishmael was a refugee and there hung over him at all times the refugee's bitter sense of deprivation.

When, in 1948, the Egyptian radio exhorted its Arab brethren in Palestine to flee the country or stand the risk of being killed in a war that was about to be launched against the Jews, Ishmael, his mother and sister left their home in Jaffa and fled to Damascus. The loss of his home and livelihood was rendered all the more bitter by the fact that his two elder brothers, sceptical of Egyptian promises to liberate their country and passionately attached to their lands, had stayed behind and prospered.

'You could have knocked me down with a feather Mr Crawe.' (Ishmael's feelings towards Alan were such that he could never bring himself to address his friend by his

Christian name.) 'The nerve of that fellow! He didn't even bother to hide them properly. Guns galore: there under the seat and just covered by a few old sacks. I couldn't believe my eyes.'

Alan thrust his fingers into the mouth of a jar and clutched a handful of black olives; shaking the oil from his fingers, he began to slip them into his mouth. 'It's your own damn fault, Ishy. I told you that man was no good. I told you to get rid of him. Would you listen to me? He drove like a maniac and looked like a gangster.'

'Oh, Mr Crawe. Everyone you meet these days looks like a gangster, particularly Syrians.' He let out a feeble laugh.

'I told you not to take on a Syrian. If one of our drivers is going to get into trouble, let him be Lebanese, then his own people can deal with him.' He bit an olive in two and let it lie on his tongue, stewing deliciously in a mouthful of arak. The agreeable sensation that filtered through his body as a result of these combined flavours softened his temper. 'Of course, that's the end of the Damascus trips for the moment,' he said more mildly.

'Oh, Mr Crawe!' cried Ishmael. 'I promised Mother I'd be in Damascus next weekend.' His mother lived in Damascus with relatives, and Ishmael always worked hard to keep the Syria–Beirut trips well booked so that he could spend a few days every month with her – he was a devoted son.

'You should have thought of that before you hired that Damascene thug. I told you to take on a Lebanese.'

'Oh, you're perfectly right! Why didn't I take your advice? Why didn't I? I could kick myself. The trouble with me is I'm as soft as butter. He spun such a yarn. You should have heard it. You can't trust anyone these days. Everyone breaks the law, murdering people, and betraying their friends. It's awful. Sometimes I feel I'd just like to get right away and start afresh. To London or somewhere.' He stopped, a look of utter dejection on his face.

It was a round, unlined, well-padded face. A happy face, though when his features were in repose his dark eyes were surprisingly melancholy. Alan felt sorry for him.

'Cheer up, Ishy! It's all over! Here's to freedom!'

Ishmael raised his glass of arak and drank, but the toast only depressed him further. 'You know, this whole thing has thoroughly upset me. I don't mean being nabbed by the police, although you can't trust those fellows to be fair with you once they start throwing their weight around. If they don't want you to be innocent, then you just aren't. I know. But suppose they catch the fellow, suppose he puts the blame on me.' The very thought of such an eventuality put him into a panic and he dropped his head in his hands with a little moan.

'Be your age!' said Alan kindly and patted his friend's wide shoulder.

It was at this point that the doorbell rang, and Ishmael, whose imagination had evidently been embroidering on the idea of the driver's perfidy, looked up with a little cry of terror.

Alan went to the door and opened it, to find Sarah standing on the threshold. Her large blue eyes looked up at him with their customary expression of truculent appeal. 'May I come in?'

Sarah shook hands with Ishmael but did not catch his name, which was drowned in the blast of a wireless set from across the courtyard. She sat down on a couch facing the verandah. She felt rather light-headed with excitement and hunger, for she had had nothing to eat since noon. And now that she was in this comfortably untidy room with its framed drawings, quantities of books, and tumbled cushions, she felt happy.

She took it for granted that Alan would help her. After all, he was English and a man. And there was a reassuringly firm and determined look about him – a quickness of movement and decisiveness of feature.

She came straight to the point. 'Mr Crawe, that man, this morning. Do you know that his name is Colonel Raschid Ahmed?'

He nodded. 'I heard it over the news.'

'I've just had a letter from him.'

'But he's dead.'

The shine died out of her face and she stared at him dully. His words shocked her like a deliberate cruelty. The dead cannot communicate, yet Colonel Ahmed had sent a message to her, and in doing so, had lived again.

'I'm telling you what happened,' she said coldly. 'Will you read it, please?'

She took the letter from her bag, handed it to him and sat watching his face while he began to read.

Colonel Ahmed had written to her in English.

Dear lady

You have told me that you are distressed for the need of money. I too am distressed for need of help and I turn to you in my need.

This morning, before we met, I had been trying to find a man, Emile Khalife, for whom I have important news of the gravest nature. But too late, I have discovered that this man has left Beirut and is residing for the moment in a village in the mountains. I am afraid, indeed I am certain, that I will not be able to reach him. I have therefore written him a letter, and I earnestly beseech you to deliver it to him. It will take you no more than three hours to reach this place which is called Chakra and which you will get to by going first to Baalbek. I think it better for you to join a tour, for if you go alone you will be conspicuous and may be followed. Also, do not go to the police for they can be bribed. If you fail or feel yourself to be in danger, go to your embassy, but only as a last resort. In Baalbek hire a taxi to take you on the road to Chakra which is sign-posted and begins at the Jupiter temple. When the land begins to rise you will come upon a fork in the road and a sign post. Take the right-hand road that will bring you to Chakra. On no account take the left-hand road and watch for yourself and your safety. I should die of self-reproach if any harm should come to you.

As I write this I look up and see you sitting opposite me and all the words that you have spoken to me go once more through my mind. I know you will not humiliate me by refusing to take the money that will be given to you. It is not payment, as there is no way of arriving at a price to be put upon this task. You can call it a gift in return. You have told me that you need money and I know of no other thing to give you.

Now as I write this the thought comes to me that perhaps you would prefer to do this for me without reward. I cannot tell for I have not had sufficient time to study your mind.

Yet I am tormented by doubt, for you have told me that you have a great deal of pride and this leads me to examine the question carefully and distresses and confuses me. So you must forgive me if I blunder. The important point is that I do not wish to be under an obligation to you, for obligation is a barrier and when we meet again I would like it to be without debts on either side.

And now, gracious lady, goodbye, and may Allah protect you.

With respectful compliments
Raschid Ahmed

Alan read the letter through and put it down on the table, from where it was taken up again and read by Ishmael. Sarah paid no heed to this; in fact she did not even notice. She watched Alan, eager to catch every sign of the letter's effect upon him. She felt that something momentous hung in the balance, and that Alan was about to arbitrate in a matter of great importance. It was not just a question of whether or not she should do what Colonel Ahmed had asked her – this was of secondary importance, and she had long ago made up her mind about that.

Alan, though he did not fully understand the letter, was angered by it.

'What's this money he's talking about?' he asked brusquely.

Sarah told him what had happened. She spoke in a deliberately flat, calm voice for she saw that Alan disliked the letter and she did her best to suppress her excitement. She told him again of the telephone call in the café when Colonel Ahmed had allowed her to think that he was talking to the police, and of the man who had brought her the money in the university garden. 'I think it must have been a brother. There was a strong likeness. He has a brother, I know. His name's Tawfik and he has a business in the Avenue des Francais.'

'How much money?'

'About . . . five thousand Lebanese pounds.'

Double that, thought Alan. At least she has the grace to feel ashamed. 'What an underhand trick,' he broke out furiously. 'Getting you mixed up in a sordid political quarrel, bribing you to run his errands for him. What is this letter he wants you to deliver? Who is Emile Khalife?'

'The people I'm staying with say that someone of that name has an important position in the Lebanese security police.'

'Someone of that name! You must know that Khalife is an old Lebanese family. There are Khalifes scattered all over Lebanon and Syria. You chose a convenient profession for your Khalife. He's much more likely to be some Lebanese bandit the Syrians are financing. Before you know where you are you'll be shot or jailed for treason. This, what's his name, Ahmed, you can see the sort of man he is, bribing you with a small fortune and then getting himself killed before you can refuse it.'

Sarah's face grew tight and obstinate. 'He wasn't bribing me. He didn't have any choice. There was no one else to turn to.'

'You're not going to do this idiotic thing?'

'Of course I am. How can I refuse? Besides, I need this money. It's a godsend. You wouldn't want me to take the money and not deliver the letter would you? That's what his brother thought I was going to do. He despised me. I don't blame him.'

Alan stood up and was pacing about. 'I'll give you the money,' he shouted at her rudely. 'Give that back. How much do you want?'

But she felt absolutely committed, not by the subtle machinations of Colonel Ahmed, but her own romantic nature. Colonel Ahmed's letter had filled her with pride. He had called out to her, from the very grave; there was something miraculous in this. She had been set alight. It was unthinkable to extinguish happiness with cold doses of caution and commonsense.

'I can't take your money. This is different. It's a debt. You read what he said. But if you'll help – I've got to get to Chakra tomorrow. It's about fifteen miles from Baalbek. I looked it up in the *Guide Bleu*. There's a Roman temple there – I expect people go quite often to look at that. I thought if I went as a tourist, in one of your cars, so as not to look conspicuous, in case the men in the taxi saw me with Colonel Ahmed this morning . . . it's possible someone might be watching me.'

'I'm glad you can at least see the need for caution, Miss Lane.' He leaned over her. 'Don't get mixed up in this! Don't you understand? A man's been murdered. You were with him. Have you listened to the broadcasts from Cairo today? Do you suppose these political manoeuvres are some kind of game?'

This was more or less what Sarah did think, and with good reason, for almost everyone else thought so too. Violent and bloody though the Middle East might be, it was also richly fantastic; and for those with a turn of sardonic humour, even comical. How could one take seriously rulers who one moment were advocating the assassination of neighbouring monarchs, colonels and presidents and in the next embracing with fervent vows of friendship their prospective victims? The world of *The Arabian Nights*, where a queen escaped death by story-telling, might have put on modern dress but clung to its accustomed ways, and the Arab people, for all their striving towards nationhood, remained imprisoned in their own fantasies. Even violence, by following antique patterns, was for her not as shocking as it ought to have been, and when it was learned that the male members of a mountain village had swung the scales of vendetta by killing a dozen of their traditional enemies from the village in the next valley, the news came to foreigners in Beirut from afar – from two hundred years ago, or even further. It was hard to realise that real people were actually at that moment suffering as the result of such unnecessary, uncontemporary crimes.

'Mr Crawe.' It was now Ishmael who spoke. 'I think we ought to help Miss Lane. She's in a spot, you know. You're perfectly right in a way. I don't think she ought to go off on her own. It would be much better if one of us took her.'

'Shut up, Ishmael!'

'Please go on, Mr Ishmael,' cried Sarah. 'You're very kind. Will you take me to Chakra?'

'Why not, Mr Crawe? I'm taking those people to Baalbek tomorrow. I could easily go a bit further.'

'Do you want to be shot?'

'Oh *pouf!* We're much more likely to be shot in the suks. Or run over by a taxi.'

'This *is* a sudden attack of courage,' said Alan sarcastically. 'Two hours ago you were in jail weeping with terror.' But seeing Ishmael's round face fall forlornly, he turned away, ashamed of himself. No man likes to be reminded of such moments – Ishmael, who longed to be brave, least of any.

'Don't listen to him, Miss Lane,' cried Ishmael. 'I don't care two pins for those bullies! As for being scared of taking you to Chakra, well, you can count on me. This is just between us, Mr Crawe. You don't need to have anything to do with it.'

'If you go to Chakra tomorrow, I'll report this conversation to Inspector Malouf and have you both arrested.'

Sarah could only gasp with dismay and Ishmael cried, 'Oh! no, Mr Crawe, you couldn't do that! Miss Lane came to you for help. She trusted you. It would be absolutely rotten to give her away.'

Alan knew he was behaving badly – shouting, losing his temper, insulting Ishmael – but he felt desperately, illogically, against this enterprise. He made an effort to control himself, sat down opposite Sarah and addressed her earnestly. 'Miss Lane – Sarah – if there's nothing wrong with this man, if he's not asking you to do something dangerous and subversive, then there's no reason on earth why you shouldn't give those letters to Inspector Malouf.'

'Inspector Malouf!' cried Sarah. 'All he wants to know is how many men I've slept with. And you read what Colonel Ahmed wrote about them. How do I know he's not just as dangerous? Did they catch the men in the taxi? They didn't even ask questions about them. That's the whole trouble here unless you know who you can trust.'

'Why trust this Syrian?'

She leaned back on the divan, shrinking a little into its cushions. My blood trusts him, my heart trusts him. 'I trust my own judgement – we talked – I found out a lot about him.'

'What's a Syrian doing in Lebanon getting himself shot at?'

'Please don't shout at me. I don't see why you dislike a man you don't even know. It's obvious what happened and they want something to set it off. They don't like Colonel Ahmed. He's always wanted Syria to be friendly with Lebanon, and he's very popular with the army. They wanted him out of the way so they killed two birds with one stone. But he knew what they were up to and got in first. I bet you, if we opened this letter . . .'

'Then why don't we? Let's put your improbable theory to the test. Let's open this letter and see what it says.'

'I couldn't do that. He'd think I didn't trust him.'

'Good God, woman! He's dead!'

'How do you know?' said Sarah calmly. 'I've spoken to two people this afternoon and both of them said he is alive. I hope he isn't dead. It's lucky he isn't dependent on you for his life.'

'I'm only trying to make you see reason.' She's mad, he

thought. Another eccentric English woman with illusions of grandeur. History was thick with them. Lady Hester Stanhope galloping about in turban and trousers, Gertrude Bell dodging Turkish officials all over Syria, Sarah Lane the girl who stopped the revolution. No wonder the Arabs are sick of us. It's time we stayed home.

'Mr Crawe,' said Ishmael. 'I think Miss Lane is absolutely right. I admire her sense of honour. Why can't she come with us tomorrow?'

'No, Ishmael! No! No! No!'

Sarah got up abruptly. 'Thank you, Mr Ishmael, for your kindness. Good night, Mr Crawe. Please don't bother to see me out.'

'I'm sorry.' He spoke stiffly, for he felt ashamed. Not for having tried to dissuade her – he believed sincerely that he had been right advising her to hand the letters over to the police – but for not having been honest in his reasons.

Sarah pressed the lift bell, but no lift came to her summons. She assumed it was out of order, though what had happened was that a Saudi Arabian on the fifth floor had left the door open so that the lift would be waiting for him if he should want to go out, a practice that was indulged in by most of the people in the block for reasons of convenience for themselves and revenge upon their neighbours.

Sarah therefore descended the stairway, treading carefully to avoid pieces of orange peel and melon rind that had slopped over from garbage tins; the garbage collectors, either excited or intimidated by elements in the present crisis, had not been on their rounds that morning.

She had reached the ground floor and was approaching the short flight of steps that led into the street when she heard footsteps on the stairs behind her, and the sound of someone calling her name brought her to a halt.

'Miss Lane! Miss Lane!' Ishmael, puffing with exertion, hurried across the foyer toward her. 'Please wait.'

The foyer was dark, for the globe in the light that was usually kept burning there had been broken some weeks before by revellers returning late from a party. The bottom steps were lit by the street light. Ishmael did not come down them, but hung back in the shadow. His hands twisted one within the other, nervously.

'I'll take you, Miss Lane,' he whispered. 'You come along tomorrow at nine o'clock. I'll take you.'

'But can you? Won't Mr Crawe be there?'

'Oh, he never goes on these trips. He can't bear tourists.'

A car slid by and though Sarah could not see his face, she had the impression that he watched it in the way people whose minds are distraught stare at some insignificant thing nearby, longing to escape into it from themselves.

Why does he want to help me, she wondered. For Ishmael's manner suggested a desperate boldness, and alarm bordering on terror. Was it pure perversity because his friend had opposed their going, the kind of impulse that makes a Beirut motorist plunge on against the stop signs? Or had her adventure fired his imagination? Perhaps he liked her for championing Colonel Ahmed, and for being stubborn, foolhardy and courageous, all qualities with which the Arabs were abundantly endowed and which they admired when they came across them in other people.

'He said once,' Ishmael continued in an abstracted voice, 'that if he had to listen to one more American saying it was just like California, he'd shut up shop and go back to London.'

But as Sarah smiled he became suddenly agitated. 'Don't misunderstand me, Miss Lane. I'm absolutely devoted to him. If it hadn't been for Mr Crawe I don't know where I would be now – penniless and in jail at that – twice. Except it would only be once because I'd still be there from the first time. You know what the police are like once they get their hooks into you. I could never repay him for what he's done, but you know, a man wants to call his soul his own.'

Another car swept past. Ishmael stepped back. She saw his plump form recede into gloom by the lift. He hesitated, then turned and hurried up the stairs.

CHAPTER 9

Everyone conversant with romantic literature knows well that the muezzin, that beautiful haunting call that rings throughout the Muslim East, rouses the sleeper from his morning couch. The occupants of the Hanouches' house had little hope of defying this tradition, for the mosque in an adjoining street was liberally fitted with loudspeakers, and the voice of its Iman bawled relentlessly through their open windows.

Sarah lay for a moment, listening to this melodious din, then got up and dressed.

She found Mrs Hanouche in Nadea's sitting room listening to the early morning news from Cairo. The old lady sat on a divan near the window, a cup of coffee precariously tilted and clattering in its saucer as her hand trembled, her head inclined slightly toward the wireless set, which gave out a spate of truculent Arabic from a green profusion of potted ferns. Sarah could not understand the commentary but she could see that it displeased Mrs Hanouche, who scowled, and every now and again emitted exclamations of indignation. After a few moments the news was given in English.

'Arab brothers, people of Lebanon, what are you waiting for? How long will you continue to suffer under the yoke of the criminals that rule you? Only yesterday another hero and martyr of the freedom-loving Arab peoples, Colonel

Raschid Ahmed – that jewel in the forehead of the peace-loving Arab nation – was shot down and trampled in your streets, was murdered and spat upon by cowardly Arab haters under the thumb of the imperialist gangsters . . . Arise!'

'The assassins!' cried little Mrs. Hanouche, her coffee cup trembling violently in her had. 'The liars! The filthy liars! Listen to their lies, Mademoiselle Sarah. What is to become of us? What can we do? These murderers will cut our throats while we sleep in our beds. Forty years I have lived in this house, forty years.'

Sarah rescued the coffee cup. 'Is there anything in *L'Orient* about Colonel Ahmed?'

But Mrs Hanouche was too excited to take the question in. 'You hear what they are saying, Mademoiselle Sarah? There are fanatics in this country. This is the kind of encouragement they want. There was a time when if people wanted to attack us they had to send armies in to do it. People think twice about that. It's a big step, and even maniacs hesitate to make it. But they can go on day and night stabbing us to the heart with this monstrous weapon, this diabolical invention.'

Sarah was turning over cushions looking for the morning papers. '*L'Orient* –'

'There is no morning paper,' cried Mrs Hanouche. 'They threw a bomb through the window last night. All the papers are on strike. The suks are closed.'

From what window a bomb had been thrown and where Mrs Hanouche got this information from, Sarah could not find out, for the old lady was too excited to offer rational explanations, but it proved in part at least to be correct; there was no morning paper.

The strike, however, had not yet extended to Rhas Beirut and there was little to inform the casual observer what direction events were taking. Sarah, leaving for the travel agency a little before nine, stepped out into a brilliant morning. The sun, shining as though in defiance of dark events, touched with a satin sheen the new vine leaves in the Hanouches' garden and burnished the green skins of watermelons in the stall across the road. The only evidence of the crisis was in the still-uncollected garbage spilling over from dustbins onto pavements and into gutters.

She was not the first of the Baalbek party to arrive: two Frenchmen equipped with a quantity of cameras, tripods and photographic gadgets were already waiting by a large red car outside the agency office, and Nigel and Margaret Thorne, also with cameras, were approaching from the opposite direction.

'Hello, are you coming to Baalbek too?' called out Margaret in a tone of evident relief.

Oh, damn! Those ghastly English, thought Sarah. 'I thought you were leaving,' she said.

'We are. We've got seats on the Monday plane. But it seemed such a pity to miss Baalbek and they said in the hotel there was nothing to worry about. Though I don't know. Coming along in the tram . . . I wouldn't go in a taxi . . . and on the street corner . . .'

'Margaret, it was only a friendly argument,' put in Nigel, looking down at her indulgently.

Sarah noticed this glance and the tender look with which Margaret returned it. So they are in love, she thought and ceased to resent them. She looked around her, impatient to set off. Where was Ishmael? What were they waiting for?

'As a matter of fact,' Margaret confided, lowering her voice, 'we were rather forced into this. Last night we rang up to see if Mr Ishmael, that's the guide who's going with us, was still in jail. You remember yesterday we told you how he had been arrested because the police found guns in the back of the car? Well, he answered the telephone himself and persuaded us into this trip today. I wasn't very keen with everything so unsettled, although of course I want to see Baalbek, but Nigel didn't want to give him the idea that we hadn't any confidence in him after what had happened. These people are terribly sensitive.'

This latter pronouncement embodied Margaret's new approach to the Middle East; she was not disliking it any the less, but a new tenderness between Nigel and herself had made her anxious to accept his views, which meant doing them justice. She was essentially a serious person, constantly examining her ideas of right conduct; she wanted to know what ought to be done, and then to do it. Nigel's attitude to the world around him, his eagerness to take it all on his own shoulders, she felt to be noble and unselfish. She wanted to emulate him – not because he was Nigel, but because he was right. They had had a long serious talk about it in bed the night before.

'We are ambassadors, Margaret,' he told her, as he tentatively caressed her thigh. 'The future rests with people like us. If you and I can't show these people that we like and respect them...'

'But I *don't* like them' she told him. 'Perhaps other people can like them – I'm sure you do – but I can't. I like people to be sensible and unemotional and orderly. They have all the qualities I don't admire.'

Nigel closed his eyes, a way he had of ignoring a remark that he did not want to answer, but as it was pitch dark this manouvere was lost on his wife. 'Understanding and tolerance...' he continued, and drawing a little closer, moved his hand over her belly.

Margaret's flesh jumped nervously under his fingers. 'Well, why can't they be tolerant of us?' she asked breathlessly.

'Why should they? They have every reason to hate us.'

'But it hasn't all been our fault. I was reading that history of the Middle East last night and it says that if it hadn't been for the quarrel between Egypt and Transjordan, the Jews would never...' But as Nigel's arm encircled her she began to lose the thread of her discourse. 'I forget exactly what it was, but anyway the Egyptians behaved abominably.'

Nigel did not want the blame portioned out. He had claimed the lot and could not bear to give any of it up. 'Of course, after centuries of foreign domination . . .'

'But that was the Turks, not us,' murmured Margaret.

They left it at that while they paused to make love and were too sleepy afterward to continue their discussions. But at breakfast next morning Nigel, recollecting that Margaret had had the last word, reopened the conversation, supporting his case with quotations from the *Short History of the Middle East*. These had been carefully underlined so he was able to put his finger on them quickly, and Margaret, who had read the book with an open mind and not marked anything, was unable to put up an adequate defence. She allowed herself to be persuaded and set out that morning fortified by a solemn vow to be tolerant and understanding.

This new resolution had, however, been quickly shaken. The tram ride had been a mistake. There had been an incident on a street corner near the American university. Over the heads of the small crowd she had seen two men swinging their fists about, the gleeful little boys, the two indifferent police; moreover the tram itself had been dirty, crowded and, according to a fat man seated on her right, possibly contained a concealed bomb that might explode at any moment, scattering on the road dismembered passengers.

By the time they reached the agency she was wishing they had never set out. How much more pleasant to be back in the hotel, in bed with Nigel. They could have made love again. Memory swept over her and soothed her. She looked at Sarah and, informed by her new experience, thought, She's in love too, and then, without envy, How beautiful she is!

'I wonder what's holding them up,' said Sarah. 'It's hot, isn't it? Let's get into the shade.'

They drew into the shadow of the agency doorway and, as on the day before, Sarah, turning her back upon the street, looked at the photographs displayed in the window.

Her gaze moved heedlessly from one to the other – from the six famous columns of Baalbek to the palace at Beit ed Din, to the source of the Adonis River at Akfa. An impulse moved her, as in response to vague, uneasy premonition, and raising her eyes she looked beyond into the shadowy interior of the office.

At the back of the room by the big office desk a man was standing, looking out at her.

Surprised, but not alarmed, Sarah stared back at him. He did not look away, indeed he seemed hardly to realise that he had been observed, imagining that the office window shielded him from view, and something in his expression made her feel that he had been watching her for some little time. He looked desolately sad and frightened. Good God! she thought. It's Ishmael!

Recovering from her astonishment, she smiled. Abruptly he moved forward, putting out a hand to open the door. It swung open and he came out into the sunlight in all his plump, happy, perspiring reality, a reality so unlike the watchful, sad-eyed man gazing through the office window that she could hardly believe she had seen him there and put the encounter out of her mind.

'Hello! Hello!' he cried. 'Hello, Mrs Thorne! So you found your way all right. We'll be off in a jiffy.'

'Oh, yes, thank you,' said Margaret. 'But, Mr Ishmael, are you sure it's all right to be going to Baalbek? I mean, what about the crisis? Someone in the hotel was saying it's one of the spots where there's always trouble because of being near to Syria.'

Ishmael laughed. Far from being unhappy, he was excited and gay. 'Don't you worry, Mrs Thorne, we'll look after you. That's our job. In any case, nobody in this country is going to do anything to tourists in Baalbek. It's the biggest thing they've got.'

'But there are a lot of Muslims in the Bekaa.'

'Mrs Thorne, I'm a Muslim and I'm not going to eat you.'

'Oh, I didn't mean that!' said Margaret, blushing furiously.

'Oh, she didn't mean that!' cried Nigel.

'What I mean is,' said Margaret, 'don't the Syrians feel that the Beka'a ought to belong to them, so that whenever there's any trouble –'

'Mrs Thorne, Baalbek doesn't belong to the Muslims or to the Christians either, or to the Syrians or the Lebanese. It belongs to you.' He ended grandly, 'And to Miss Lane, and to the Anglo-Lebanese Travel Agency.'

'It belongs,' Sarah put in, 'to Jupiter.'

'By Jove,' cried Ishmael. 'That's rather good. It belongs to Jupiter! I say, did you hear what I said? By Jove!' Laughing immoderately, Sarah thought, at his own witticism, he wheeled about and hurried over to the two Frenchmen. Soon he called out to them, 'Come on ! We're off now. I'm going to drive because that fellow disappeared, you know, and in any case we've sacked him. Will you all hop in?'

Everyone moved over to the car. The Frenchmen and their photographic gear took up most of the back and the Thornes chose the centre seats. Sarah had just taken her place in front when the agency door opened a second time. Alan came out of it. It swung to with a crash behind him. Standing on the pavement, his hands on his hips, he regarded the party with an expression of bitter irony. He showed no surprise in seeing Sarah – he must have been watching them through the window, as Ishmael had watched, a moment before. She waited, wondering what he intended to do. Surely he would not dare order her out of the car. She gazed at him with an expression at once defiant and supplicating.

She was right in her guess. Alan had been watching them for some moments from the office and had been wondering whether or not to interfere. He had expected Sarah to be there; when Ishmael hurried out the night before, he had guessed that it was to make some arrangement with her about the trip to Chakra, and he had come into the office that morning in the certainty of seeing her. At the time he had only wanted to verify his guess. But when he saw them together he became angry and felt he hated her. She looked so fresh, so vivid, so expectant. Her smile wounded him with its insolent happiness. She looked radiantly beautiful and this radiance at such a time seemed a point she had scored against him.

He turned angrily to Ishmael, who, caught out in guilt, rushed for the car and, scrambling into the front seat, gripped the wheel.

'Ishmael!'

'Right ho! Mr Crawe,' gasped Ishmael. 'We're all set! We're off now. Everything's ready.'

Abruptly Alan made up his mind to go with them. Beyond this resolution his intentions were vague – his motives also. Had he set out to thwart the wishes of this romantic Syrian, this figure which, even as a ghost, so far outshone him? Or was he protecting an ignorant girl from her own folly? But there was not time to establish the validity of his impulses, even had he wished to do so, and as it happened he preferred not to go into these rather delicate questions. He simply told himself that somebody responsible ought to go along and keep an eye on things. He even indulged in the exasperated reflection that such responsibilities always fell to his lot. Why did he have to chase around cleaning up Ishmael's messes? Why was it always he who had to be unattractively cautious?

He strode over to the car and, thrusting his head through the window, spoke to Sarah. 'So you're going on this wild goose chase?'

'Yes, I am.'

Alan opened the door. 'Move over, Ishmael. I'll drive.'

'But –'

'Hurry up!'

'But you're not coming!' wailed Ishmael.

'Hasn't it penetrated your thick head that I am? Get over!'

Ishmael swung a fat leg over the gears and edged himself nearer to Sarah. He bent his head to hide a quivering face.

They set off and for the first five minutes or so no one spoke. Sarah, indignant for Ishmael and fearing a possible setback to her plans, turned her head away from Alan and looked out of the window. The Thornes, sensing tension around them, maintained an embarrassed silence.

The big car turned down Avenue Bliss and along the Corniche past the swimming clubs. On the red dunes, where the evening before Sarah had seen a grey stallion prancing on the sand, stray donkeys wandered and dogs nosed about in the rubbish dumps by the nomad camps. A few stunted pines, beaten into slanting growth by the wind, stood here and there on the smooth, gently curving billows of sand. The road was practically deserted and a blind beggar kneeling beside it, his silvery eyeballs raised to the glare of the sun, looked saintlike in his loneliness.

Ahead the mountains rose up, their snowy summits hanging high above the warm, torrid plain. At the foothills the car turned northward and, taking a narrow lane that led through banana plantations and groves of bamboo, crossed the Beirut River. The party began to look about with interest and the tension relaxed between them. The Frenchmen enthusiastically discussed a Roman aqueduct and Margaret ventured to put a question to Alan that she had been longing to ask for some time.

'Excuse me, Mr Crawe, but when you spoke a moment ago of a wild goose chase, did you mean that we ought not to be going to Baalbek, because of the crisis, I mean?'

'Oh *really*, darling,' murmured Nigel.

'If I thought you shouldn't be going,' Alan replied tersely, 'I wouldn't be taking you.'

Only partially reassured, Margaret leaned back in her seat. Nigel felt for her hand, but the superior note in his voice had annoyed her and she drew it away. She looked out of the window and tried to take an interest in the scenery. How delightful it was! she told herself. The pretty farms, the children picking flowers at the roadside, the loquat trees tied up in huge brown nets. Yet somehow it was not as delightful as it ought to have been. She felt irritated and on edge.

On the turn-off into the Damascus road they ran into a line of fast-moving traffic and police patrols every few miles or so. The first of these waved them through, but they eventually fell victim to a patrol stationed outside a café a few miles from Aley.

Everyone had to get out, Sarah with a nonchalant air that was far from reflecting her feelings, for she had just remembered that she had no passport and that Inspector Malouf had told her not to leave Beirut. The officer in charge, however, being a Muslim, looked upon the two women as politically nonexistent, waved them aside and occupied himself with questioning the men.

Sarah strolled to the edge of the road and stood looking down over the neat bushy tops of umbrella pines to the orchards and vineyards below. In the distance the buildings of Beirut shimmered, pearly and brilliant, but on the mountains all was sharp, hard and dry. Thorn bushes and spiny thistles growing at the roadside stood out rigid and delicate as though etched on the bright air. Someone called out, 'Come on! We're going,' and the sounds hung in the air, clear and thin, as though rounded and polished by the sunshine.

Sarah turned to find Ishmael standing behind her.

Staring at me again, she thought. What's the matter with him?

'We're going,' Ishmael repeated mechanically.

Sarah spoke abruptly. 'I suppose he's told you that you can't take me to Chakra.'

He looked away down the stony slope. 'What did he want to come for?' he said sadly. 'Why does he have to interfere? It's none of his business.'

They turned and began to walk back to the car where the rest of the party stood waiting. 'It's only that it's going to be more difficult,' he said in a low voice. 'We'll have to wait for an opportunity. You won't go off on your own?' he added sharply. 'Keep your eyes on me. I'll fix it. You promised!'

It did not occur to Sarah, as they got into the car, that somehow the tables had been turned, and that it was Ishmael who had promised to take her to Chakra, not she who had promised to go with him.

Again they set off, pulling out into the road to join the long shining serpent of cars that coiled up through orchards and vineyards to Aley and Sofar on the higher slopes above.

Although it was still early in the season, the annual migration from the coast had begun and crowds were already thick in the Aley streets. Sarah did not care much for Aley – she could never imagine why the Beirutese went there when they could just as profitably have stayed at home. She supposed it was some ancient racial habit, instinctive and irresistible, like the migrations of birds, that sent them rushing up every summer from the coast. For it was perfectly evident that the mountains offered little of interest to them, apart from altitude and the enjoyment of driving at high speed round dangerous corners. Nature, they believed, needed improving, and there were as many cafés, casino and modern hotels in Aley, Sofar and Brummana as in Beirut itself. Indeed, if it had not been for the cool air and for an occasional glimpse of pine forests between the tall houses, one might have been in Bab Edriss or the Avenue des Francais.

Ishmael, on the other hand, thought highly of Aley; there was nothing he liked more than spending a summer weekend in this gay, noisy place. But this day he was too preoccupied to pay much heed to it.

The car slowed up to pass through the thronged streets; he did not even notice where they were. The town was full of shouting taxi drivers, the blare of horns, radios playing in open cafés; he heard nothing of this. He sat between Alan and Sarah, staring blindly before him, and Aley passed as in a dream. Memories, vivid and terrifying, possessed his mind.

He was still living in the night before, in the still, dark hour between eleven and twelve. A small bar in a narrow street near the Hotel St George, the atmosphere dim with cigarette smoke, a jukebox playing softly in the corner, the fat Damascene leaning forward, his elbows on the table . . .

Ishmael shuddered as he remembered the Damascene.

His name was Fuad. His round, smoothly shaven face shone as though rubbed with coconut oil. He picked his teeth meditatively with an ivory toothpick, all the time watching Ishmael, his eyes like half-shuttered windows, the thick brown lids hanging over them. He rarely said anything, rarely moved; but sat, heavy, lethargic, picking his teeth. Ishmael was terrified of him.

He was not nearly as frightened of Fakhr, though Fakhr had twice the brain of Fuad. He could tell that to look at him. His narrow, bony face was sensitive with intelligence; he suffered from conjunctivitis and his eyes were always blood-shot, but they looked straight at you, disconcertingly, with an expression of penetration and contempt. It was Fakhr who only two weeks before had held a knife at his throat and threatened to kill him if he didn't go on; and it was Fakhr who had first threatened him six months ago in a café in Damascus, saying, 'Help us to get the Jews out of Jerusalem.' Yet still he was not afraid of him as he was afraid of Fuad. For something told him that if ever it should come to the point and they did kill him, as they sometimes said they would, it would be Fuad who would do it, who would stand up slowly in his lethargic way and stab him in the breast.

But now I'm finished with them, he thought. Now I'm finished! He had bought his freedom from them the night before with the last desperate venture. A gust of hope rushed over him, bringing the blood to his cheeks and filling him for an instant with sweet, false joy.

He looked down and saw Sarah's knee beside his own, the yellow linen of her dress drawn tight across it. Her naked arm touched the sleeve of his coat. That morning he had looked at her and felt anguish for his victim, in all her youth, warmth and beauty. Now he had no feeling about her. He did not think of what lay ahead. He pursued his destiny blindly, fortified by an unquenchable hope that something at the eleventh hour would intervene between him and disaster. And just as, six months ago in a Damascus café, he had cast barely a thought to the possible consequences of his actions, so now, full realisation of what he was doing awaited a future moment, a final, inescapable, dreadful revelation yet to come.

It is a fact of Middle Eastern life that men seem often able to escape just retribution for their follies and crimes. Fate, in the very moment of punishing them, suddenly drops them, as though bored at the last moment with the notion of justice. So it happens that murderers go free, conspirators are captured and released to conspire again, and bad men, their crimes still freshly printed on their foreheads for all to see, sit cynically in high places. This amiable tolerance toward the wrongdoer, so clearly manifest all about him, had kept Ishmael well infused with optimism in the past and sustained him now.

Something would happen to protect him – something would turn up. The very insecurity of life provided a safeguard against private disaster. He might be caught and put in jail but, then, before they could do anything to him, there might be a revolution, or a war – the Syrians might invade Lebanon, or the Egyptians – or even the Jews.

CHAPTER 10

At eleven they had reached the Beka'a and were driving swiftly toward Baalbek. Already in the distance the celebrated six columns – all that are left standing of the fifty-four that once enclosed the Temple of Jupiter – stood out, tall and distinct from the surrounding fields.

The town from this distance showed as a mere smudge on the hills behind and the six columns stood alone commanding the plain. But as they approached nearer, the town became articulate, its flat mud houses set on the bare hillside of the anti-Lebanon. They could pick out minarets, winding lanes and stone walls. The hills behind became mountains patterned with snow drifts and the sliding purple shapes of cloud shadows; these looked westward across the wide green valley to the other mountains – the Lebanon itself – higher, more massive and more deeply locked in snow.

Those of the party who had not seen Baalbek before drew a breath of wonder, for now the ruins appeared so huge they were out of scale with everything but the plain on which they stood and the mountains on either side. The mud houses of the town were abased by the enormous ruin, and the poplar trees growing in dense groves at its foot looked like silver-stemmed, green-leafed rushes.

Conversely the mountains, though they dwarfed the town, could not dwarf the ruins. The huge rosy columns, the massive broken walls towered up above the tops of the poplar trees, to stand against a blue sky and against the tawny, ragged flanks of the anti-Lebanon. Those who had built the temples had matched them against their inspiring situation; the great shafts of rose-gold stone, the enormous lintels and carved capitals stood displayed against a background of natural splendour, comprising an entrance hall, a majestic introduction to sky, snow and mountain.

The road followed the outer wall of the acropolis and came to a wide open area outside the main gate. Here Alan stopped the car and everyone got out, to be instantly importuned by a camel driver offering rides on an attendant beast, and a dealer selling fake Greek coins. Small ragged boys swarmed about the car and, making instinctively for its most vulnerable occupant, fastened upon Margaret; one, carrying a black and white kid, wanted money, presumably for looking charming; another thrust a half-dead flower into her hand and begged payment for this. Alan brushed them away and swiftly shepherded his party through the temple enclosure.

'If you want to take photographs, take as many as you like in here,' he told them. 'But don't photograph the town. The people don't like it.'

'I don't want to photograph the town,' said Margaret. 'It doesn't look very interesting and I expect it's filthy.' The boys by the car had set her nerves on edge.

The two Frenchmen threw off their coats, an operation which brought to light brightly coloured sports shirts, elaborate with tucks, pleats and buttons and, hurrying through the propylaea, quickly set up their tripods in the main courtyard.

Sarah, sauntering close behind them, listened with respect to a lively discussion concerning such matters as composition, shutter speed and reflected light; her association with Marcel had done little to eliminate her English awe for the French language and this particular conversation, though quite innocent of profundity, sounded obtuse and learned to her ears.

'Je vous en prie, Madame, mais passez donc – Vous êtes dans ma photo,' called out the younger of the two, a slender young man with a blue shirt and hair clipped across the top like a newly cut lawn. Sarah moved out of the way and entered the other Frenchman's picture.

'Alors, quand même pas dans ma direction!' shouted this enthusiast impatiently.

She left them and made her way over the ruined court, where in the heyday of the Heliopolitan Jupiter worshippers gathered before the steps of the great temple, and in the surrounding sanctuaries the gods of the Roman world looked out from two hundred and fifty niches.

The sun, which as Jupiter and Hadad-Baal had reigned on this spot since before the days of Solomon, still possessed it. The sky flung its light upon the court as into a receptacle fashioned to receive it, and burned there at such intensity that even the shadows bloomed a warm, tawny gold. The six columns, towering up from the massive platform that had been built to support the Jupiter temple, glowed rose red – their shadows lay across the floor of the temple so emphatically that Sarah's instinct was to leap over each one, as across an impediment.

There were quite a few people about – tourists from Europe and America who, determined to snatch some intellectual benefit from their visit, went about book in hand, or clustered around hoarse-voiced guides. Only the Lebanese took Baalbek lightly and, making no attempt to master its archaeological mysteries, climbed around the walls happily, or chased pretty young women around pillars and under doorways. They were used to Baalbek. They had lived with it for over two thousand years and looked upon it principally as a good place for a picnic.

By the eastern wall of the Temple of Jupiter a broken stair led down from the higher level of the temple itself to a courtyard below; this was flanked by a row of columns that earthquakes had toppled from their pedestals, the huge shafts still lying in a debris of broken pieces.

Sarah sat down on a stone within the shadow of the wall and watched the rest of the party trail up the long flight of steps into the Temple of Mercury. They formed a straggling group, its units separated, she supposed, by incompatibility or anger.

The Frenchmen went first, side by side and talking volubly. Then came Margaret, walking alone, Nigel a short distance behind her.

They've had a quarrel, thought Sarah. She was not surprised. She was beginning to like Margaret. The girl seemed honest and sincere and Nigel had made affected remarks about Baalbek, calling it vulgar, comparing it to Hollywood and the wide screen, which must have tried her patience.

Alan and Ishmael brought up the rear. They were talking to each other excitedly – at least Ishmael was excited, judging by the way he waved his arms about. She saw Alan's head turn for an instant in her direction before they disappeared into the temple.

'Oh, don't worry,' she murmured aloud. 'I'm still here and what can I do with you hanging onto Ishmael by his ears?'

The sun had made her sleepy. She leaned back and the warmth from the hot stones behind her seeped into her body. Yellow flowers with sage-green leaves dabbled their shadows on the temple wall and lizards that looked as hard and desiccated and ancient as the stones lay rigid in the sunlight. She watched them drowsily. She felt relaxed, comforted, her excitement of the early morning subdued by the heat. She glanced at the Temple of Mercury, half expecting to see Ishmael hurrying down the long stairway, but Ishmael and the rest of the party had disappeared.

A short distance from her a man was kneeling on the ground trying to measure the girth of a fallen column with a dressmaker's tape measure. Sarah watched himidly.

That he belonged to the Middle East there could be no

doubt. The sun shone on his black hair and brown face. He was dressed in a khaki uniform liberally decorated with brass buttons, ribbons and snow-white lanyards; field glasses and camera dangling from his shoulder kept impeding his efforts to adjust the tape measure; a shooting stick leaned on the column shaft beside him. He applied himself to his task eagerly, without reserve, whistling noisily through white teeth and every now and again giving little exclamations of annoyance as the ends of the tape measure slipped from his fingers. He seemed not to think it possible that he might be watched or to consider the need for concealing his smallest feelings. Sarah thought he looked like a goat – like one of the black, blunt-headed, mad-eyed Lebanese goats that seemed to have survived from the youth of the world.

He looked up and saw her watching him. 'Madame! Madame!' he called. 'Please help me! I cannot get these two ends to stay together.'

She went over to him and put her finger on one end of the tape measure. He wound it around the column and noted the measurement in a small black book. 'I am a journalist,' he explained, when this was done. 'I have to be accurate in my profession.'

She looked at the card he gave her and handed it back. 'I thought you were in some army or other.'

'No! No!' He touched the lanyards on his shoulder lovingly. 'A uniform is always useful, it gives one authority. Iranian boy scouts, first class.' They regarded each other solemnly, and it was the Iranian who burst into a peal of laughter.

Sarah smiled. 'Are you working for an Iranian newspaper?' she asked.

'No! No! I am writing a travel book. One moment!'

Putting the notebook and tape measure away, he took from another pocket a rather larger and much-handled volume. 'This is my last book. It is about a trip around Turkey.' He opened it to display smudged type and a murky-looking photograph just recognisable as himself. 'It is called *Nightingales and Roses*. I would like to give you this book as you have shown such interest in my work, but it is the only one I have left. I brought fifty copies with me, but I have had to give them all away.' He put the book away and, jabbing his shooting stick into a crack between some stones, sat on it decisively. 'And now, Madame, tell me your impression of this big ruin.'

Sarah paused for thought. 'Well –' she began.

But the Iranian had already burst out angrily. 'You see! You see that!' He pointed to fallen columns and broken capitables, a yellow butterfly hovered on the carved eyelid of a stone lion, palpitating its wings. 'That is the fate of all colonialists! Even the butterflies fly higher.'

Sudden and oppressive, like a wave of pain, boredom came down upon Sarah. She yawned and looked hopefully toward the Temple of Mercury.

'Why do we come here, Madame?' demanded the Iranian excitedly. 'Look! Look over there!' He pointed. Behind the Temple of Mercury the houses of the town showed clustered on the slopes of the anti-Lebanon. Here and there a green belt of trees, the minaret of a mosque, stuck up above the flat roofs and mud-coloured walls. 'There are the people. It is a plot. These travel agencies, they are all in league! You know, they are all under the thumb of the Americans. Do they take us into the town and show us the aspirations of the people? No! No, never! It is Roman temples everywhere!'

He paused, breathing deeply. 'I shall go!' he declared suddenly, and standing up snapped together the expanding seat of the shooting stick.

'Good idea,' Sarah encouraged him. 'You know there's a most interesting mosque in there. You shouldn't miss it. It's on the pound note. Or is it the five pound?' She opened her bag and took out her wallet, but the Iranian was impatient to be away, bowed swiftly and hurried off.

She watched him go without regret. He had unnerved her a little by sounding a particular note just when she had been feeling thankful for its absence. For it had come to her mind some moments before that one of the remarkable things about Baalbek was that no picture of Gamal Abdel Nasser or the Virgin Mary had been stuck up on it.

As Sarah herself had remarked that morning, Baalbek belonged to no one, if not to Jupiter himself. Like all ancient monuments, it was in a sense immutable, beyond the reach of conquest and political ferment. Here, politics did not matter. A few hundred yards off in the streets of the town the mosques might resound to the cries of angry imams, the pulpits tremble to the eloquent priest, but the ruins had passed beyond all this contemporary fuss and persisted, serene, in the rarefied atmosphere of their long history.

With the Iranian gone, this atmosphere once more reasserted itself. The sunlight palpitated on the golden court; the yellow flowers hung over their inky shadows; the lizards lay rigid or flicked like lightning into their holes. And Sarah waited, bemused by the sunshine and forgetful for the moment of Ishmael, of Alan, even of Colonel Ahmed.

A faint cry called her to herself. She looked up to see the party trailing out from the Temple of Mercury.

They had lunch by a café set in a grove of walnut trees just outside the town, a cool green spot watered by the spring to which Baalbek owed its existence. When everyone had rested, the Frenchmen said they would like to look at a shop that was reputed to sell coins and other antiquities.

This was situated in the centre of the town and looked out on the main street with its incessant parade of camels, donkeys, sheep, goats, assorted pedestrians and lurching, travel-stained buses; a haze of dust and smoke hung in the air, dulling the sunlight; from a café across the street a loud-speaker poured political speeches and Arab film music into the ears of the populace.

Inside, the shop was small and dingy and offered to the eye an oppressive confusion of modern 'arts and crafts' –

brass hookahs, wooden camels crudely carved and varnished, leather slippers and bags painted with pyramids and sphinxes. A few pieces of broken pottery and pearly Roman glass, some Greek coins, nearly all suspiciously identical, and Phoenician beads comprised its stock of antiquities.

'How much do you want for this?' asked Nigel, holding up a chipped Roman lamp.

The dealer, who was fat and dark-skinned, and seemed, like a Rembrandt portrait, to melt indistinctly into the gloom around him, stood miserably torn between two conflicting desires – to do business and to insult an imperialist warmonger. For the crisis in Beirut had had the usual effect upon the emotional temperature of Baalbek. The town seethed with angry rumours, and passions ran high. He stared at Nigel sullenly. 'Fifty pounds,' he replied at length.

Nigel put the lamp down in disgust. 'This fellow doesn't want to sell,' he said to Sarah, who stood beside him, fingering a length of Damascus brocade.

'Offer him a price,' said Alan. He felt a little uneasy and was anxious to get his party away from the town. He had parked the car in a side street behind the shop and wondered now if this had been wise. There wasn't much they could take, apart from the windscreen wipers and hubcaps, but they could always puncture the tyres. He brushed the thought away. They know me here, he told himself. I've brought them plenty of business. But the atmosphere was too tense for comfort; some unsavoury remarks shouted by street urchins had followed them into the shop.

He leaned over the counter and spoke to the shopkeeper in Arabic. 'Ibrahim, send your boy round to keep an eye on the car.'

Ibrahim nodded and turned to shout an order over his shoulder into a dark room behind him.

They had always been friendly. Alan had known him for two years; had brought him many customers and never given the show away on the fake Alexanders. After all, if people were silly enough to buy fake coins, that was their affair. Once Ibrahim had invited him into the room behind the shop and given him some arak. But today his manner was sullen and he kept his eyes averted.

'Mr Crawe.' Ishmael touched his arm. 'Did you lock the car?'

'Yes.'

'Are you sure? I don't think you did, you know. Can you hear that broadcast? It's just as well to be on the safe side. People were saying some pretty nasty things when we went past.' He lowered his voice. 'There was one chap who called me an imperialist stooge. Did you hear? If I hadn't had these people with me, I would have walloped him. Give me the car keys. I'll just slip round and make sure.'

Alan, his attention divided between the broadcast, Ishmael and the unsmiling eyes of Ibrahim, absently handed over the keys.

At the other end of the counter the Frenchmen were inspecting the Alexanders, going over each one with a magnifying glass. Having had some experience of French thoroughness, Alan suspected they would be there half the afternoon and then would buy nothing. He wondered whether he should tell them to hurry up but decided against it.

He was not in the least worried for himself. It was these others, these innocents abroad, you never knew what they would do. Frenchmen, he had learned from experience, were as passionate in argument as the Arabs, and Nigel belonged to that class of Englishmen who looked insolent by the simple accident of his countenance. The only one of the group whom he felt he could count on to behave herself in a ticklish moment was Sarah. She would not, he felt sure, precipitate an incident. He looked around the unsuspecting party, watchfully.

Margaret had moved to the door and stood looking out into the street. In the café opposite a group of men in white kaffiyehs and brown robes were sitting around tables, drinking coffee and smoking hookahs. They were beautiful, she decided, their features strong and proud, their eyes flashing under jutting brows. The white head-dresses formed a perfect frame for their swarthy features and even the ugly ones suggested a nobility of thought, so that one credited them with great endurance and courage. They argued together, their faces vivid with feeling, heir hands tracing the theme of their talk with swift, expressive gestures.

Yes, they were beautiful. They were worth coming to see. But as for the rest of the place –

Dirt, dust, noise, chaos – somehow, she thought, you could tell it was a Muslim town. The flies, the sullen black-eyed youths, the shabby shops, the squalling wireless sets – and a sense of anger and profitless resentment brooding like an undercurrent to the confusion and noise.

It is for this, she thought, that we back down and make way? Dirt and anger, beggars hanging around for baksheesh, people always wanting something for nothing, whining children giving you flowers you don't want and then asking to be paid for them, tormenting you into charity. She thought of Jupiter's temple, the dignity and calm within the spacious court and it seemed the antithesis, and her own inheritance.

She was aware that she was committing some large fault in understanding. Nigel could have told her all about it. She did not care; she did not want to understand. She had taken sides now in a conflict as old as Baalbek itself, and prayed that the heirs of Hellas might triumph over the Orient.

When Nigel, relinquishing his lamp in disgust, came to her side, she did not turn to smile or look at him. She felt intensely irritated – with Baalbek, with Ishmael for having persuaded them to come, with the whole excursion, Nigel included. She could have wept with disappointment, for the day had started so well. They had awoken that morning in the same bed, really in love for the first time. What had happened? What had gone wrong?

The tram ride, those two men fighting in the street, the horrible children by the temple . . . How could Nigel pretend to like these things when he hated them as much as she did? All his love and tolerance was only theoretical, a mere attitude of mind. This compassion for something large and unspecified, something you never had to face – what was it but a substitute for true affection, and the only way out for those with little heart?

Margaret deeply regretted having come to the conclusion that the English were the only acceptable people in the world and England the only place to live. She knew well how unattractive this view would appear to their friends at home. But there she was, and that was her conclusion. At least I'm not fooling myself, she thought, and despised Nigel, who, it seemed to her, was.

At that moment, during this fresh crisis in Margaret's relationship with her husband, the Iranian appeared, walking down the street towards them.

The sunlight gleamed on his satin black head and sparkled on the brass buttons of his uniform; the white lanyards swung to the rhythm of his stride. People, impressed by his military appearance, stood back to let him pass; dogs and children trailed at his heels as though part of a retinue.

Nigel recognised him first. 'Look! Isn't that the Iranian journalist?'

The Iranian advanced jauntily. Jabbing the point of his shooting stick into a piece of melon rind that happened to be in his path, he flicked it dexterously over his shoulder.

'Oh, my God, no!' cried Margaret.

The Iranian burst into ecstatic greetings. 'Hello! Hello, Mr Thorne! Hello, Mrs Thorne! So we meet again. You have been visiting Baalbek? And where is your friend, Mr Green?'

'He didn't come,' said Nigel.

'And what do you think of Baalbek, Mrs Thorne? It is not so remarkable. We have better things in Iran.'

Margaret, taut with dislike and determined not to answer,

turned away from him. Yet when it came to the point she was not quite able to be entirely rude but sought instinctively for some way of cloaking the snub. The café across the street caught her eye; the men she had admired were still there, drinking coffee, smoking and talking. Remembering dimly something she had wanted to do a moment before, but for some reason had refrained, she took a step out into the street and fumbled for her camera. Raising it to eye level, she snapped the shutter.

The whole street erupted as the men from the café, with cries of rage, rose up and hurled themselves upon her. She saw, as in a nightmare, the tall menacing bodies, their robes billowing like sails around them. Someone snatched the camera from her hand and dashed it to the ground, stamping it into the dust and kicking it in fury. Others closed around her. She felt their hands, hot and greasy with sweat, fumbling on her body, dragging her arms. They shouted at her, so close she could feel their breath on her face, gesturing with their hands at her very lips as though to pluck contrition from her tongue.

It had all happened too quickly for her to feel afraid; but she felt sick and revolted. Not so much for the contact of these strange male bodies against her own, but for the scene's ugliness, the shouting and cursing, the stumbling about in the dust. She could hear dogs, roused to excitement, barking in the street. She heard herself shouting too. 'Take your hands off me. Leave me alone! Nigel!'

'Here!' cried Nigel, who had rushed forward and was struggling toward her. She saw his white, strained face, his long arms flung out to catch her hand. Their fingers touched, but were plucked apart. 'Leave her alone . . . She didn't mean anything! It's all a mistake!' he shouted.

Ishmael, who had just come back from the car, Alan, Sarah and the two Frenchmen rushed out of the shop.

'Keep back!' cried Alan to the younger Frenchman, who was eagerly hurrying to save the lady from distress. 'Don't be a fool! You'll only make it worse. Ishmael, keep them back in there. Get back!' he ordered Sarah and pushed them into the shop.

'No! No!' cried Ibrahim, whose family – a fat wife, five children and an old grandmother – now filled the shop to overflowing. 'You cannot stay here! They will pull down my shop! They will take my things! You must get out and not come back.'

'Don't be a fool!' said Alan and, thrusting twenty pounds into Ibrahim's hand, hurried out before the man had time to think.

He had half expected to see Margaret and Nigel torn to pieces, but the ardour of the attack had abated a little. The crowd was larger, children had come running from all directions and people from the nearby shops pressed forward to see what was happening, but they now seemed less interested in the Thornes than in the Iranian, who was yelling at them at the top of his voice and flinging his arms about in declamatory gestures.

As the crowd grew quiet it became possible to hear a little of what he was saying. 'Do not be hasty,' he begged them. 'You have been insulted, it is true, but do not forget the laws of hospitality. These strangers are standing upon the threshold of your homes. They have been rude and stupid, but that is not their fault. They cannot help themselves. Is it not better that you should forgive them?'

A few of the older men murmured angrily. The Iranian flung out his arms. 'Remember!' he cried, 'America has atom bombs. They can drop them on your town and blow you into little pieces. You are weak and unprepared.'

'We will not give them any more oil.'

'We will cut the pipelines!' shouted a fanatic here and there. But the majority seemed impressed, not so much by the Iranian's argument as by his eloquent delivery and frequent use of striking metaphor. He now began to quote appropriate passages from his books and they nodded and murmured appreciatively at some particularly felicitous phrase. It was evident that a poet had come among them – they forgot Margaret and Nigel and were prepared to listen to him for the rest of the afternoon.

Seeing them attentive and comparatively quiet, Alan gently elbowed his way to where Margaret stood, trembling and dazed, wiping the dust from her lips.

He knew he ought to feel sorry for her; he wanted to say something gentle and reassuring. Instead he burst out, 'You bloody little fool! Didn't you hear me tell you not to take photographs?'

'I'm sorry,' she said pathetically. 'I didn't think. It was on the spur of the moment. I had no idea.' She shook the hair back from her eyes and seemed to recover a little. 'How childish! How ridiculous! Grown men! Just because I took a photograph! They've absolutely ruined my camera! Where is it?' Her voice shook with anger. 'It's brand new. We bought it in Germany when we came through. They ought to be made to pay for it!'

'*Madame!*' cried the Iranian, who had heard this. 'Please be calm! You are a stranger here. These men could break you in two like this – crack! crunch! And feed you to the pariah dogs! Here is your camera!' Someone handed it to him. He blew at it and rubbed the lens energetically on his sleeve.

Nigel limped towards them, brushing dust from his trousers. 'Well, it is childish,' he said in his high voice. 'We haven't done anything. They ought to be made to understand how foolish that kind of behaviour is. Why, all over the world . . .'

'Oh, for God's sake!' said Alan and, taking Margaret firmly by the arm, led her to the café and made her sit in a chair. She sank limply into it and was suddenly sick.

'I'll get you a glass of arak,' said Alan gently. 'It'll buck you up.' But he was more worried about Nigel, who was still arguing with the Iranian. 'Mr Thorne,' he called out. 'Don't be a fool! Keep your voice down, smile and if necessary apologise.'

'That is it,' cried the Iranian, who seemed to have changed sides and now argued the Arab point of view excitedly. 'You are continually insulting them! First you take pictures of them and then you will not apologise.'

'But that's the whole point,' said Nigel. 'I'd apologise gladly, but there's nothing to apologise for. We haven't done anything to offend anyone. We're perfectly friendly. We have absolute good will for everyone.' He had a logical mind; the whole situation was ludicrous and he simply had to explain this. 'Look, make them understand. It isn't an insult to take photograph. It's a compliment. My wife wouldn't have photographed them if she hadn't been interested in them. In London people photograph the Queen. She doesn't mind. She likes it.'

'Your Queen is beautiful,' said the Iranian. 'She wears diamonds. These men are not beautiful. It is an insult.'

'Mrs Thorne,' said Alan, 'will you tell your husband not to be a fool.'

'Nigel!'

'Just a moment, Margaret,' said Nigel. 'But that's absurd,' he continued to the Iranian. 'We photograph them because they – well in a way they are beautiful. And they interest us.'

'Why? They are none of your business.'

'Qu'est–ce qui se passe?' called out one of the Frenchmen from the doorway of the shop.

'Get back!' shouted Alan.

'We like them,' explained Nigel, 'because they are different from us.' The Arabs, few of whom could understand what he said, shuffled closer around him, peering watchfully into his face. 'We like things that are different. It would be boring if everything were the same.'

'Aha! You admit it!' cried the Iranian. 'You want to keep things for yourselves. You grind them under foot! It interests you that they sit here in the dust with dogs. Nobody built a road for them. You see the temple that the Romans built. Why did they not build roads for the people?'

'That's just what they did do,' said Nigel patiently. 'Nobody built better roads than they did. And what's that got to do with taking pictures?'

'These men sit in the dust wearing old-fashioned clothes and no hats. They put white cloths on their heads like desert barbarians when they ought to wear hats in the modern way like we do.' The Iranian smiled suddenly, as though aware, all in a happy rush of feeling, of his superiority to the Baalbek Arabs; but in the next moment his face had darkened with anger. 'You photograph them and print their pictures in newspapers and mock at them.'

'But that's ridiculous.'

'It does not matter!' cried the Iranian, suddenly beginning to shout with excitement. 'You must respect the customs of the people. Here it is the custom not to take photographs. There is supposed to be a revolution starting. Perhaps, who knows, it is starting here. You never can tell. Why did you not ask their permission? Aha! That is it!' He turned and addressed the company.

The Arabs listened to him attentively. At length a few shadowy smiles appeared. One of the older men began to order people around and at his direction the men lined up into two straggling rows and shuffled closer together.

'What are they doing?' asked Margaret hysterically.

'I think they're getting ready to have their photographs taken,' said Alan.

She burst out laughing. 'Please control yourself,' he said sharply. 'That wasn't funny!'

'Don't I know it! The filthy brutes!'

In the meantime other people hurried up to be photographed. Urchins came running, but the original group wanted to keep the company exclusive and shouted to them to go away. At last they were ready, each man standing to attention and looking glassily into the distance.

'Now, Madame, they are ready!' said the Iranian. 'Now you can take a picture and please give them a copy afterward.'

'Not if it kills me!' cried Margaret.
'Madame! You must not insult them by refusing.'
'I'll take it,' said Nigel quickly.
'*Et moi aussi!*' cried out both Frenchmen, hurrying forward with their tripods.

Alan looked back at the shop, in sudden recollection. Leaving Margaret, he hurried across the street. Ibrahim, his wife and five children filled up the doorway. He pushed past them into the shop. Ibrahim's grandmother sat in a corner among wooden camels and leather slippers, talking to herself. Ishmael and Sarah had disappeared.

'Where are they?' He grabbed Ibrahim by his fleshy shoulders and swung him round. 'Where are the lady and Ishmael Qazzaz?'

Ibrahim shook himself free of Alan's grip and, moving slowly past him, took his place behind the counter. 'They have gone.'

'Where?' The ugly scene in the street outside had established a mood, seemed a preface to disaster. 'Where did they go?' he shouted.

Ibrahim, his expression sulky and obscure, merely shrugged his shoulders.

CHAPTER 11

———

Ishmael and Sarah left the town by way of a narrow lane that wound between low stone walls. On either side poplar trees, growing close and slender, bent to the wind like ripe barley and in its fitful gusts burst into a flurry of silver; the air was filled with their rustling and with the ripple of water from innumerable hidden streams.

Ishmael drove fast, swerving to avoid occasional goats, chickens and children, and for some time neither of them spoke. Sarah was feeling a little ashamed of the way in which they had abandoned the rest of the party, but there had been no time to think. A moment ago she had been sitting in Ibrahim's shop trying to make out what was going on outside; then Ishmael had grabbed her by the hand whispering, 'Hurry, Miss Lane! I've got the keys. It's now or never. It's your only chance!'

The lane led them out onto a broader road that pointed straight across the valley to the mountains. At this point the Beka'a begins its slow ascent toward the plain of Homs, where the Orontes rises in a gush of crystal waters; but the climb up onto the northern plain was not here perceptible; the valley was mountain-locked, inviolable; the great ranges enclosed it in an immense peace and isolation. Cloud shadows brooded over a patchwork of fields, the green of wheat alternating with the dark red and purple of ploughed land; and the valley looked so sumptuous in its vivid colours and the thick plush of crops, that the mountain slopes, dressed with little but thorn bushes and boulders, seemed to be plunging down into some softer, richer element swathed at their feet.

Ishmael increased his speed; and still no word passed between them. The Baalbek party and their troubles had drifted out of Sarah's mind and a curious despondency possessed her. She would have found it hard to say why, but now that she was doing the very thing that she had wanted to do, she felt sad. It was so simple after all. Influenced subtly by Alan's cautiousness, she had come to believe that Emile Khalife at Chakra was a long way away and that a long time and a great deal of trouble would be spent in reaching him. But now they were almost there. In another twenty minutes or so they would reach Chakra. Then she would ask to be taken to Emile Khalife, she would give him Colonel Ahmed's letter, and that would be the end of it.

Colonel Ahmed only lived through the task he had imposed on her and by completing it she would condemn him to extinction. Already, as they drew nearer to the mountains he was losing substance in her imagination. Death had already claimed him.

Suddenly Ishmael burst out, 'Miss Lane, do you ever feel that you're just so fed up with everything that you'd like to get away – right away from everything you've ever known and start your life all over again?'

She looked at him in surprise. He sat beside her, gripping the wheel and staring at the road ahead of him. There was a look of such suffering on his face that she felt shocked, as though she had looked up to find a stranger sitting in his place. 'Of course, everyone feels that sometimes.'

'You know, I lived six years in London. Dear old London! I wish I could go back. I wouldn't mind what I did, just to get out of this place. Miss Lane, you don't know what it's like. Nothing can ever be the same again.'

'Don't you think it's like that everywhere? And this country is so beautiful.' She looked out over the splendid valley, lying calm as a lake, and peaceful, with the snow peaks glittering above it. The fields through which they were now passing were divided by rose hedges covered in pink blossoms, and peasant women wearing black head shawls and long skirts of red and purple were picking the roses, stuffing them into sacks and loading them onto donkeys. 'What are they doing with all the roses?' she asked.

'They take them back to their villages,' replied Ishmael in an abstracted voice. 'They make scent out of them. It's quite an important industry.'

The sight of the women plundering the rose hedges moved Sarah deeply and introduced the feeling of unreality that was to claim her. She wondered what was troubling Ishmael. She knew nothing about him, and wondered if he was a refugee who had been driven from his home and from fields and orchards similar to these. She felt inexpressibly sad for him, and sad because she carried a letter from a dead man in her handbag. 'After a year,' she said, 'you'd be so homesick you'd have to come back.'

'You know, Miss Lane,' said Ishmael, after a moment's silence, 'I'm Palestinian, if you can say you're something that doesn't exist anymore. I said that to an American last week and he said, "Now, you know, I'm a bit vague about all this, just exactly where is Palestine?" "It isn't anywhere," I said. We had a house and land in Jaffa. You should have seen our orchards. You should have seen our oranges, Miss Lane. The oranges they grow here are like walnuts compared with ours. Then the Jews came. The British were there and they did try and stop them after a bit, when it was too late. Nobody could stop the Jews – they just came – and more and more and more of them. And then those damn Egyptians. They told us that if we didn't get out we'd be killed because they'd be dropping bombs on us. So out we went, my mother and Georgette and me, and did they drop bombs? Not on your life, they didn't. And the Syrians and the Lebanese – they said we were martyrs and heroes and all that rot – they were going to do everything in the world to help us, and do you know what they did? We got to the Lebanese border. It was ten o'clock at night and it was cold. They helped us all right. They gave us cups of coffee and made us pay for them afterwards. Three times what we'd have had to pay in Beirut. That's how much help they gave us. Sometimes I wish I'd stayed behind with the Jews. My two elder brothers did and they've done pretty well for themselves. They told me I was a fool to listen to Radio Cairo and I was.'

'Well, why don't you go back? It's not too late.'

'What's the good? Miss Lane, if I went back and the Egyptians ever did go in, they'd shoot me on the spot.'

'But you're all right now, aren't you? I mean you've got the travel agency, and you like Alan –'

'I'm devoted to him. I'd do absolutely anything for him. But, you know, he doesn't understand me.'

She looked up at him. He stared straight ahead and the sun, striking full on his face, glittered on the tears in his eyes.

It was then that she began to feel afraid. Why was he crying? Why was he talking like this?

Yet what was there to be afraid of? Nothing had happened except that they were driving a little faster; nothing alarming had come into view.

On their right they were passing a small village, its mud houses long and flat, and shining white, with patterns in soft bright blue, the blue of the Virgin's robe, painted around their doorways. A Christian village. There was the square church with a rounded arch over its door and a belfry topped with a small white dome. A caravan of donkeys trotted along the road ahead of them, bells tinkling on their blue bead collars and Hessian sacks loaded on their backs. Every now and again, from a split in one of these sacks, a pink rose dropped to the ground. It was quite a long caravan and they slowed up to pass it, for it was taking up most of the road. A man walking in front turned a handsome, swarthy face towards them as they passed.

The land began to tilt toward the hills. Wheat fields and poplars, the red Beka'a tulips, nomads with their goat–hair tents – all this in a matter of moments was behind them. They entered a world of white rocks and wild lavender. They passed the first stone house commanding a few acres of heroic terracing, the house and the terraces hardly distinguishable from the barren slope out of which they had been fashioned. Behind the houses, high up on a cliff face, goats patterned the sun-drenched rocks like strings of black beads; there was no one in sight but the shepherd who watched them.

Ishmael changed gear for the ascent. One would have thought that he was taking the hill on foot, for he was out of breath. Sarah saw that his round face glistened with sweat.

A wilderness was closing around them. No one seemed to live on these barren westward slopes of the mountains. Sarah's perceptions were playing tricks with her and the hot, dry desolation of the landscape affected her strangely, as though their way were leading her into danger, when in fact they were travelling swiftly and comfortably to Emile Khalife.

Emile Khalife. Even this name rang with a new resonance. Who was Emile Khalife?

It was beyond belief! Only two days before she had left Marcel, vowing sternly to be wiser in the future, and an hour later a handsome stranger had only to look at her, to speak softly, to plead. Would her fatal susceptibilities always override her judgement?

Then ahead of them was a sign post and the road forked. Ishmael turned his wheel and took the left hand road.

'No,' said Sarah. 'This is the wrong way.'

Ishmael increased his speed. 'Mr Ishmael stop! This is not the way to Chakra.'

'Miss Sarah, I know every stone of this country. I have driven tourists to Chakra many times.'

'Stop! Stop!'

Ishmael stopped and, changing into reverse, shot back to the sign post.

'There,' he said. 'Read that.'

The arm of the sign post pointing left carried the word 'Chakra.'

As she looked at it for the first time her trust in Colonel Ahmed faltered. The loss of her trust was sad and heavy like bereavement. As with Marcel, he had made a fool of her. She also regretted not having trusted Ishmael. She was shocked and disappointed, feeling that Colonel Ahmed had betrayed her. It was not until later that she remembered that the signpost had been newly painted; perhaps on that very day. And this error in judgement, and bereavement, confused her.

In the meantime Ishmael again took the left-hand road and she glanced at him, wondering if this was the time to apologise.

'Mr Ishmael, I'm sorry.'

'It's perfectly all right,' he said. 'Don't worry, everything will be perfectly all right.'

The road turned again. Fifty yards ahead a group of big grey boulders hung over it like the posts of a ruined gateway and, from behind these, six men stepped out into the centre of the road. Their kaffiyehs were drawn over the lower part of their faces, swathing their heads so that only eyes and nose were visible; heavy leather bandoliers crossed their bodies; they carried rifles. One man advanced ahead of the others and held up his hand.

Ishmael slowed the car to a standstill and they crowded around it.

'Who are these men?' cried Sarah. 'What do they want?'

As though impelled against his will to look at her, Ishmael turned. His lips trembled. His face was haggard and drawn. 'How – how – should I?' he gasped.

One of the men opened the door and stood silently beside it, waiting for him to get out. Ishmael shouted at him in Arabic, then slid around in his seat, kicked out with both feet and lunged forward, driving his head into the man's chest. Two men sprang forward and, grabbing him by the arms, hauled him from the car. Sarah watched as they dragged him to the side of the road and threw him down. He flung out an arm toward her.

'Miss Sarah, don't worry . . . These bullies!'

They closed around him. Broad backs and flapping Lebanese trousers hid him from view. She wondered what they were doing to him; whatever it was, it must have been instantly effective for there was no sound from Ishmael.

She felt curiously unmoved by his fate. Perhaps some reservation in her mind neutralised compassion; perhaps she was numbed by surprise. Yet was she surprised? For the past five minutes or so, for a reason that she could not now remember, she had been expecting something like this to happen.

I must hide the letter, she thought; but there was no chance of doing so now, for the men were coming back to the car. The tallest of them, the man who had grabbed Ishmael, came and stood by the window and looked in at her. His face, or all that she could see of it behind the swathes of white cloth, was dark, brick red; the eyes piercing blue.

She had not yet fully accepted what had happened. By one of those unpredictable tricks of the imagination she saw the scene and herself in it with detachment, as though these things were happening to someone else. She stared calmly into the face of the blue-eyed man. 'What do you want?' she said in English and then in French. The man did not answer, but jerked his head at her as an indication that she should get out of the car. When she did not move he took hold of her by the wrists and dragged her out. 'Let me go! I can get out!' He let her go and she stood on the road, her legs suddenly soft with fear.

They're going to kill me now, she thought. Like Ishmael. She looked across expecting to see his body huddled on the side of the road, but a group of men still hid it from view. She did not need to see him, her imagination informed her and, drawing upon her store of violence, she remembered Colonel Ahmed and the old man in the French suk crawling about among his broken, blood-coloured flowers.

But she was not to be killed or, at any rate, not at that moment. Two of the men took hold of her and led her down the road away from the car. She struggled to shake herself free. 'Leave me alone! I can walk on my own!' But they insisted on holding her as though to impress upon her the fact of her captivity.

Sarah upbraided them futilely. 'This is outrageous! You'll all be put in jail. The British Embassy shall hear of this!'

She did not suppose that they understood her, but she knew that people in the Middle East were impressed by quantities of words, even if they did not know what they meant. Moreover, these threats brought her a certain comfort; by mentioning the British Embassy she was made aware of all its sober strength behind her. Surely English girls could not disappear into the Lebanon, never to be heard of again.

Having shouted herself into a little false courage she fell silent. They had left the road and turned down a rough stony track that led into a valley; a little way down it a jeep stood waiting. Her captors signalled her to get into the back and crowded in after her. The jeep hurtled off like a Beirut taxi down the rough track into the valley below.

Sarah lurched against cartridge belt and rifle, but the two men on either side of her sat erect and easy as though riding spirited horses. She was beginning to suspect that they were peasants from some nearby village, not hired thugs, and looked anxiously from one to the other for some sign of friendliness. But their eyes avoided her and they did not speak to one another.

The track seemed to be leading deeper and deeper into desolation; only the stone walls dividing the small fields showed that people lived there and made some attempt to cultivate the barren land. Along the roadside purple thistles, already drying to a brittle gold, rattled in the wind. Sarah thought of Lebanon as it appears on the map, a mere strip of coast and a mountain range . . . You could drive from its northern to its southern border in a day, and from Beirut over the mountains to Damascus in four hours. Such smallness was undoubtedly comforting; yet these stark, unpopulated hills did not fit the picture, and suggested, rather, an immensity of wilderness.

Then, mounting a slight rise, they came within sight of the valley's end.

Sarah, looking out through the windscreen between the heads of her captors, saw below her a wide, shallow lake shining in the sunlight within a green girdle of poplars and willows. The flat, white houses of a town mounted the rising land on its far bank, each house set above the other in a series of such distinct layers as to appear from a distance like the steps in a gigantic staircase. Above the town, and looming solemnly over it, rose up a precipitous wall of rock, barren and treeless, its face marked with fissures and the white threads of water falls.

A quiet lake; a cliff, towering and angry like the brow of a god; summer had come late to the valley and almond and apple trees were still flowering. Sarah, looking about her, felt soothed and for a moment forgot her danger. There was something painfully strange and sweet in the gentleness of the lake discovered in that harsh loneliness.

But as they drew nearer and the features of the place became more distinct, she felt fresh alarm. She seemed to know the place, though she had never been there. She looked in an anguish of inquiry at the two sturdy peasants on either side of her, seeing them now not as chance strangers, but as people that she had been destined to meet.

She thought of Colonel Ahmed, fainting in her arms, his face pallid and beautiful. And now he lived again, through the vigour of his prophecy.

They drove along the side of the lake. The still waters

shone silver, too shallow to take the blue of the sky. The air was laden with the ghosts of gods and goddesses; here Astarte had changed herself into a fish to escape from the pursuing Typhon, and here, two thousand years ago, the worshippers of Adonis, descending the mountain road from Akfa, had cast themselves into the sacred waters. She had come to Ain Houssaine.

The jeep stopped in the village near a church. Sarah thought it ominous that no village people gathered around them while they got out; women carrying baskets of washing on their heads were walking up a lane toward them, but seeing the jeep they hesitated, and turned into an alley.

The blue-eyed man gave her a gentle shove in the back. They moved forward, crossing the street on the uneven cobblestones. They passed the church and mounted a rough stone staircase leading up into the house next door.

This was built around a courtyard and had an arcaded verandah. The dark green, pleated leaves of loquat trees shaded the steps; from a pump in the corner, water dripped into a stone basin, and a brown and white goat, speckled like a currant bun, drank from it greedily.

Crossing the courtyard they reached the shade of the verandah. A door opened; Sarah passed through it and swung around to face her captors. But the door slammed shut; she was alone.

She sank on a low divan spread with a woven rug; the room lurched and disintegrated as dizziness overcame her. She closed her eyes and fought panic.

But the moments flowed silently, smoothly by, and, as nothing happened to increase her fears, they began to recede. She looked about her.

The room in which she was prisoner was long and narrow with a high ceiling and one barred window from which she could look out onto the verandah and courtyard. There was little furniture or ornament; some couches covered with cushions, a rug on the floor, a Madonna in a small recess.

The whitewashed walls looked as clean and fresh as the inside of a shell; they were cool and uneven and friendly, and like all rough country things appealed in their simplicity. One would have expected hospitality and kindness in such a place – with the women in the cobbled streets, the church next door, the white friendly walls.

Yet Ishmael had been dragged from the car and perhaps killed by the roadside; she herself kidnapped, held prisoner.

The letter, she thought, I must read what it says and destroy it. She took it from her handbag and quickly tore open the envelope. But the letter was in Arabic. She searched the room for a hiding place, but there was nowhere that was not conspicuous.

Should she tear it up? But perhaps this was just what they wanted her to do. If the letter betrayed them and if Emile Khalife was a member of the security police, their first concern would be to keep it from falling into his hands; by tearing it up she would simply be doing their work for them.

Still undecided, she tucked it into her brassiere. Steps sounded on the verandah outside.

Well, this is it, thought Sarah. For God's sake let me keep my dignity and not behave like a cowardly schoolgirl. But her heart began to thud against her ribs and she felt stupid with fear. She waited, but the steps passed the door. A moment later she heard voices and a familiar, sharp, cracking sound outside.

She looked out of the window. Two men were seated on low stools outside her door, their heads bent over a game of trictrac.

On the bright stones of the courtyard the shadows grew longer; the sun moving slowly across to its far corner touched a pomegranate tree and lit up its brick-red blooms. The warm afternoon silence was broken only by an occasional murmur from one of the guards and the explosive crack of the trictrac counters. A woman carrying a water jar on her shoulder crossed the yard, the brown and white goat trotting at her heels. A little later this same woman brought Sarah a cup of Turkish coffee flavoured with cardamom seeds, some lebne, hard-boiled eggs and Arab bread, but when Sarah tried to question her she only smiled and shook her head, and one of the guards, a tall, burly-looking man with a drooping Edwardian moustache, stood up, peered through the window and shook his head admonishingly.

Sarah had ceased to be afraid, but a feeling of almost unbearable excitement had taken hold of her, so that it was agony – like some painful stricture of the mind – to remain in that little room, silent and alone, while somewhere outside momentous events were moving to their climax. She paced the room to give relief to her impatience. If only something would happen! she thought, when a few moments before she had been only too glad to be left alone.

Then something did happen, which, although it did not set her free, at least relieved the monotony of the afternoon and gave her something to think about. The two guards finished their game of trictrac and went away, to return a moment later with a portable wireless set. An Arabic news broadcast now blasted the silence of the courtyard. Sarah could make nothing of it though she hurried to the window and listened intently, hoping to catch a word here and there. But soon the announcer broke into French.

'Friends and brothers,' he declared, 'this is the Voice of Free Lebanon, bringing you the truth about the murder of Colonel Raschid Ahmed. Do not be put off with evasions and red herrings! The cowardly plan of the imperialist stooges has been foiled by facts and faulty imagination. The truth cannot be suppressed!

'Colonel Raschid Ahmed came to Beirut two days ago to negotiate a trade agreement between Lebanon and Syria. Things were going along nicely, but it does not suit the books of the imperialists that two Arab countries should join hands in friendship and they decided to put a stop to it. Our hearts are panting for union with our Syrian brothers, but this is not the policy of our government, which was put into power not by the will of the people but by blackmail and vote forgery. Our government is not a people's government. It is only interested in kowtowing and polishing the boots of the American warmongers and the French and British aggressors.

'This cowardly gang did not dare to come out into the open with its plots, but hired assassins to shoot down Colonel Ahmed like a dog in the streets. Being alive still when he was picked up, the police finished him off on his way to hospital.

'Last night a deputation of Free Lebanese demanded that they should be allowed to see the body of the martyr, but the President, who was in conference with his boss, the American ambassador, sent only his secretary to put these honest people off with cagey evasions. And what did he tell them? Listen to the coward's criminal words.

'He said that Colonel Ahmed was in hospital recovering from an attack upon his life by assassins hired by the Syrian government. This story is a figment of the imagination and has been exposed by the events that followed. A member of the deputation, a reporter of an outspoken and freedom-supporting Arab newspaper, did not swallow these lies. He broke through the resistance of the hospital authorities and made his way to the room where Colonel Raschid Ahmed was said to be lying. But the room was empty!

'The truth is clear for all to see! Colonel Ahmed died in the night and the murderers have smuggled the corpse out of the hospital.

'Now the whole world knows the facts of this murder and deception and a great cry of indignation has gone up from land to land.'

The guard with the Edwardian moustache turned off the broadcast and rose to his feet. In the interval of silence Sarah heard the soft clip-clop of hoofs on the road outside, and a moment later a donkey caravan led by a tall peasant made its appearance at the entrance of the courtyard.

She watched from her window. The little animals picked their way delicately up the stairs, zig-zag, to ease the strain of the climb, and came tripping forward. Bulging hessian bags swayed from side to side on their backs. Two foals, their chestnut coats shining in the sunlight, trotted at their mother's heels.

The guard stood talking with the donkey driver, then, advancing to the third animal in the train, began to unload it. Loosening the fastenings that held the sack in place, he dumped it onto the ground and slit the thong binding its top. Pink rose petals spilled from its mouth; he plunged his hands into them. He was standing with his back to Sarah, bending down, the long flapping folds of his trousers hiding the sack from view so that she could not see exactly what he was doing. He stirred the rose petals about with his hands. Then he straightened and stood erect, pulling something out of the sack as he did so.

Joseph Jemali took his sight along the barrel of a rifle, aiming it at the milky blue eye of the goat which, balancing on the top of a small water jar, was nibbling at the lower branch of the pomegranate tree. Lowering the rifle Joseph flicked a finger at the end of the barrel and dislodged a rose petal.

The donkeys stamped in the sun, twitching their long furry ears; from pools of pink roses that had flowed from the mouths of the open sacks a sweet scent, like the promise of summer, permeated the courtyard; from its perch on the waterpot the goat nibbled greedily, an expression of indifference on its ancient, satanic features; the guns lay one beside the other. Joseph regarded them with satisfaction.

Every few days for the past month donkeys carrying arms and ammunition had entered his courtyard, and out of every load a certain percentage had remained in Ain Houssaine. For the people of Ain Houssaine, who were both Christian and Muslim living contentedly together, were not sufficiently interested in the coming revolution to be tempted into it without considerable inducement.

Joseph Jemali, who now laid his chosen rifle aside to break open the mouth of another sack, was one of the better educated and wealthier men of the village and might be said to represent local opinion. A year before he had been an enthusiastic supporter of the Liberal Party, at present governing Lebanon, but recent events had brought about a change in his opinion.

It happened that a certain Salem Farid, a member of the cabinet and a distant relative of Jemali's, had been dismissed from office under circumstances which necessitated his quick removal from the country. He had taken refuge in Damascus, a city peculiarly sympathetic to discontented Lebanese politicians, and had since been bombarding his supporters and his numerous Lebanese relatives with impassioned messages urging the need for avenging his wrongs.

Salem Farid had pursued an erratic political career which had done little credit to him or his party, but the Ain Houssaine people were proud of him. The fact of their being able to claim relationship, however distant, with a member of the cabinet constituted their sole stand against obscurity; through Salem Farid they had made their mark upon the world, and, when he was dismissed, felt personally affronted.

Their grudge against the government was not, however, maintained and nurtured with sufficient passion to urge them into armed rebellion. Beirut, let alone Damascus, was a long way off. The lake, the orchards, the goats threading the stony paths, the buried treasure awaiting discovery in the foundations of Aphrodite's temple, the village in the next valley – these were the Ain Houssaine world.

For many years, indeed for as long as anyone could remember, Ain Houssaine had been engaged in a bitter feud with Chakra, the village beyond the escarpment on the rocky slopes of the next high valley. The feud began, so tradition said, in the late years of the Third Crusade, when a beautiful Chakra girl, a Christian of noble Frankish descent, was forced into marriage against her will with an Ain Houssaine Muslim. The girl's three brothers, who had settled in Chakra after many years of wandering following the break up of the Crusading armies, pretended to agree to the marriage, but at the last moment her younger brother was substituted in her place; and in the privacy of the bridal chamber this youth, throwing off his disguise, thrust a dagger into the bridegroom's heart.

There seems some doubt whether these events actually took place, and variations on this story are told by a large number of Lebanese, who have an attachment for it and like to incorporate it into their family annals; but if not from this wedding night, then from some event similar to it, sprang the enmity that exists to this day between Ain Houssaine and Chakra.

Every few years or so the feud explodes into brief and bloody warfare. An interval of surly peace ensues and then, on some dark quiet night, the brothers and sons who were killed in the last foray are avenged, another dozen men lie bleeding on the stony ground and the scales of vendetta tip to the other side.

The last raid had come from Chakra and had been a rather mild affair with only two dead, one of these an idiot boy whom nobody missed, the other, Joseph Jemali's younger brother. There had been no reprisal; not because the people of Ain Houssaine had learned the virtue of forgiveness but because the government had confiscated all arms, and they had found it difficult re-equipping themselves. Under the circumstances, a revolution providing them with quantities of arms that they did not have to pay for proved irresistible. They flung themselves into it enthusiastically, toiling long hours to rebuild the broken Roman road over the mountains so that donkeys, following the same way as the Adonis pilgrims of ancient times, might carry guns and ammunition down to Akfa and along the valley of the sacred river to the coast beyond.

Of late, however, Joseph had been suffering qualms of alarm over his part in the impending political upheaval. This Syrian, for instance, who had turned up the day before after escaping the police trap on the Damascus road had settled himself in and was now ordering people around in an offensive manner. And he was not the first. Two other Syrians had arrived a week before and installed a transmitter in the abandoned house behind the mosque. It was not that a subversive radio station troubled the Ain Houssaine people – they enjoyed listening to the broadcasts, which were couched in a language qualified to stir the coolest heart – but they were beginning to feel that they were not masters in their own village.

They had been particularly reluctant to undertake the kidnapping of the young foreign woman now a prisoner in Joseph's house; abducting women was not one of their traditional practices and if they were going to take to it, they preferred to do so spontaneously and not at the behest of overbearing Syrians. Moreover, Joseph, who knew something of the world, suspected that in this matter they might have overstepped the mark. It was all very well to fight the Lebanese Liberal party, which had insulted them by dismissing Salem Farid, but foolhardy to fight Great Britain or America; Joseph particularly did not want to fight America, where his younger sister was happily settled on a citrus farm. The Syrians had tried to reassure him by pointing out that the English girl's disappearance would not even be discovered until the revolution was well under way, by which time she would be released, and that the British would be eager to hush the whole affair up as her kidnappers would then be the established government, with whom Britain would find it expedient to come to terms. All this sounded reasonable to Joseph, and the Syrians had further assured him that they would keep on the right side of the British by refraining from burning down their embassy or, if inadvertently it should catch fire, would make swift and adequate reparation.

But supposing, thought Joseph, that the revolutionaries did not pull off their coup, what then? The majority of those who had assisted them, after handing over their arms, might be forgiven – forgiveness being a Lebanese virtue, indeed a necessity. But would Joseph Jemali, harbourer of Syrian spies and abductor of foreign women, be among them? Moreover, there still remained the unpleasant task of getting hold of that letter; suppose she should resist and declare afterward that he had assaulted her? He decided to leave this problem till the morning.

In the meantime, these reflections had so troubled him that he told his wife to take Sarah a basket of the new season's figs and a bottle of Ksara wine.

She offered them so kindly and with such a pleasant smile, on the instant Sarah knew why she had been taken to Ain Houssaine.

She was a hostage. But whose hostage? And what exchange would be made to secure her safety?

CHAPTER 12

Over an hour after he had discovered the disappearance of Sarah and Ishmael, Alan, seated in the back of a battered Baalbek taxi, was bumping along the narrow lanes that led out of the town. He had had great difficulty finding anyone who would agree to take him to Chakra. There were few road-worthy vehicles in Baalbek, and their owners unanimously agreed that Chakra was a place which, on that particular day at any rate, they did not wish to visit; only extreme financial pressures, Alan guessed, had persuaded his present driver to undertake a journey so contrary to the general inclination.

Assuming, of course, that it was to Chakra he was going, which seemed extremely doubtful for one reason and another. To begin with, would the car ever make it? With every bump in the road it seemed disposed to burst asunder. And it was already as hot as a furnace; what would the hills do to it? Well, at least it's old, he thought. It's seen more life than the usual gloomy chariot and is probably correspondingly tough. But what about the driver? Alan looked past the folds of the grubby kaffiyeh in front to the unpromising features reflected in the rear-vision mirror – the unshaven jowls hanging in sweaty folds, the bloodshot eyes, the broken tooth. Surely, he reassured himself hopefully, only an honest man could look so villainous.

They were now crossing the Beka'a and he looked ahead to see if there was any sign of the agency car, but the road was deserted. If Sarah and Ishmael had reached Chakra safely, then surely they would have been returning by now. But he had only to think of them, the trick they had played on him, and anger swept all anxiety from his mind. For Sarah his special tenderness made some allowance; he concentrated all his rage upon Ishmael. How sick and tired he was of Ishmael's stupidities! He wished to heaven he had never got caught in that fateful traffic jam, had never set eyes on Ishmael. He would break up the agency tomorrow if it didn't break itself up after this last fiasco. He could imagine the Thornes wailing and complaining at the British Embassy, party abandoned at Baalbek in the middle of a crisis and on top of that business in Sofar. Tourists would be warned off. Well, what did it matter? He was fed up with Lebanon, the Lebanese, the Jordanians, the Syrians, the Jews. He would go back to London.

'Can't you go any faster?' he shouted at the taxi driver. The man evidently put his foot down on the accelerator, for there was an enormous increase in noise, but little apparent difference in the speed at which they were travelling.

At last the road began to climb and then to wind in deep bends up the hills. The taxi made the ascent slowly, the roar of its engine an outrage in the silence. It was already late afternoon and the sunlight had lost some of its intensity; long inky shadows pointed down from rocks and thorn bushes and the hills ahead rose, sunlit, from the black gulfs of valleys.

They roared around another bend and Alan saw the agency car returning slowly round one of the sharp corners ahead.

Well, thank God, they're safe! he thought. And for a moment his pursuit of them seemed childish and hysterical. What a fool he must look in this battered taxi, like some peevish Don Quixote. He imagined Sarah laughing at him, and flushed with anger.

Then the agency car appeared round another bend. The sun flashed on the windscreen and glanced away. He saw Ishmael alone at the wheel with no one beside him.

The two cars met on a piece of straight road. A rough stone wall had been built up on the outside edge and beyond it the land dropped abruptly, too steep and rocky even for terracing. There was no room to pass and the taxi driver, keeping to the centre of the road, drew to a halt. But Ishmael, swinging his wheel around, kept moving.

'Look out, you fool!' shouted Alan. Ishmael's off wheels skidded on the loose gravel at the base of the wall; his rear mudguard scraped along the taxi's bumper bar. He jerked to a halt.

The taxi driver shouted protests and waved clenched fists at Ishmael. Alan flung open the door. 'What the hell do you think you're doing? Look at that scratch!'

Ishmael too got out of his car in a blind, fumbling way, like a man half out of his senses. He made a move to approach Alan but stopped, as though his resolution had run down like the works of a clock and left him powerless. Alan noticed that his clothes were crumpled and dusty; there was a tear in his sleeve, but he was too angry to wonder about this. A feeling of impotent rage possessed him. Sarah, where was she? The irresponsibility of the man, taking her off like that and leaving her alone. And it was more than this. He felt stifled, oppressed by Ishmael, a parasite that was sapping his strength. And the man's abject appearance only made it worse. He lashed out at him mercilessly.

'What the hell do you think you're doing? You're not fit to drive a car!'

'You will pay for this damage!' shouted the taxi driver.

'I thought there was room,' muttered Ishmael.

'You or anyone else in this Godforsaken place!'

'I'm sorry, Mr Crawe. The insurance will fix it up.'

'You should drive donkeys not cars!' shouted the taxi driver.

'Where is she?' cried Alan.

'She's gone back to Beirut.'

It was such a stupid lie he did not even heed it. 'Back your car. The road widens back there. I want to get past.'

'She told me, "I'm giving up the whole idea, to hell with that fellow!" She took a taxi.'

'Back that car!'

'Oh, Mr Crawe, *you're not going after her?*'

In a moment of overwhelming horror Alan understood. *'My God, Ishy! What have you done?'*

'She's all right! She's perfectly all right! There's nothing to worry about –' Ishmael broke off, his face quivering between terror and grief.

The taxi driver began shouting again in Arabic. 'Why does this man stand here like a camel? Get your car out of my way! Are you so ignorant that you cannot drive backward?' And to add force to the command he began to toot strenuously on his horn.

'We're not going on. We're stopping here,' said Alan, turning to him, grateful for the diversion. His head spun. He felt cold with horror. 'For God's sake, stop that row!' he burst out angrily.

The man got out of the car, slammed the door and advanced upon him threateningly. Yet, when it came to the point, he seemed uncertain where his grievances lay. 'You hired me to take you to Chakra! You are cheating me! This man ran into my car. He must pay for the damage!'

'What damage? Your car has already passed the limits of dilapidation.'

'You are cheating me!' shouted the taxi driver.

'All right,' said Alan, wearily dropping the argument. 'Don't worry, you'll be paid. Now wait over there.' Ishmael, what had Ishmael said? Sarah – No! It wasn't possible!

'You are going back on your bargain!' shouted the taxi driver.

I'll murder this man, he thought calmly. 'Shut up!' he said. 'Shut up! Shut up and leave me alone! Now wait over there.' The man, impressed by the light of menace in his eye, drew back, muttering, and Alan turned to Ishmael.

Ishmael was leaning on the car, his head on his arms, sobbing convulsively. Alan went to him and shook him roughly by the shoulder. 'Where is she?'

'She's safe.'

'Pull yourself together! What have you been doing?'

Ishmael shuddered and shrank away. Terror, grief, shame swept over him; he was half out of his mind. The time had come for confession – he saw that – there was no evading the moment. But what could he say? What had he done? What was it all about? He no longer knew. He was fighting for his home in Jaffa. That was it. He was going back. He began babbling, 'The Jews, the Jews –' but he suddenly saw that this was no good, that this would not do for Alan. Even he had never really believed it. 'They threatened to kill me,' he sobbed. 'They put a knife at my throat. If you could see that Fuad. He just looks at you. He picks his teeth. I told them I was finished. They wouldn't listen.'

'Who is this man Fuad?'

Alan spoke sternly but quietly and Ishmael, who had expected an outburst of rage, stopped weeping and raised his head. He looked about him in a dazed way, surprised to find where they were. The taxi driver sat on a stone a short distance away, chewing a piece of grass, and Ishmael, noticing him for the first time, stared at him in perplexity. Who was he? he wondered, but felt too humiliated to ask. 'I met him in Damascus six months ago. It was in a café. They started talking to me – this Fuad and a man called Nagib Fakhr. They said wasn't I a refugee. They seemed decent chaps. They said they were working to get the Jews out of Palestine.'

'You bloody fool!'

'That's all very well,' cried Ishmael. 'They said did I always want to be a refugee, and didn't I want my land back. What could I say? If I'd said to hell with that, I'm having a jolly good time in Beirut, they might have cut my throat on the spot. You can't go round saying that kind of thing, not in Damascus. And anyway I do want to go back. They said it wouldn't be dangerous. They only wanted a message carried every now and again from Damascus to Beirut. Just a piece of paper, that's all. And if I didn't do it someone else would, only it would be easier for me because I was going backwards and forwards all the time.'

'And they paid you, I suppose.'

'I didn't care about that, Mr Crawe.'

Alan believed him. No, he thought, it would not have been money that would have tempted Ishmael, but the delicious attraction of something illicit – the contempt for the stop sign on the street corner, the Arab game of making a fool out of the law. 'Go on.'

Ishmael tried to think, but his mind felt numb and foggy. He could no longer remember the slow, inexorable course of events that had led to his present misery. It seemed to him, as he tried to recall them, that at first he had been happy, that he had got a terrific kick out of fooling the Lebanese police. Could that possibly have been so? Now it seemed a hundred years ago.

'They made me carry guns. I didn't want to, but they said I was in it up to the neck and couldn't get out.'

Yes, that was it. That was when he began to feel frightened. The first, the second time had gone off all right; then he had had a near miss in the customs on the Syrian border. A new batch of police were in charge, officious bullies who had taken no notice of the fact that the ALTL was a respectable travel agency, absolutely above suspicion and part owned by an Englishman. Not content with the routine examination of passengers' baggage, they had stripped the seats off the car as well, and if it hadn't been for some trouble with a Saudi Arabian that had distracted their attention, the game would have been up.

From that day the adventure had turned into a nightmare. He had lived through each day beset by fears and had started out of his dreams at night in a sweat of terror.

'That business yesterday at Sofar,' said Alan in the same calm voice. 'The driver –'

Ishmael nodded eagerly. 'Yes, Fakhr made me take him on.'

Alan turned away; he could not bear to look at Ishmael. He hated him and hated himself for his own simplicity. He saw himself as stupid and guileless as a child. He saw depths of courage and villainy in his friend he had never suspected. In fact, this was all illusion. Ishmael remained the proud, stubborn young man who had refused to back his car for a taxi driver, but to remember this was to admit compassion and for the moment Alan had set his mind against pity. He could think only of his own grudging protective affection for Ishmael and that this had been betrayed. Looking back on the past two years it seemed to him that Ishmael had devoured the best of them – and all for nothing.

'Did it strike you,' he burst out savagely, 'that you have implicated me in your criminal idiocy? Every penny I have is in this firm. What about me? What about Georgette?'

Ishmael's eyes opened in surprise. That he should have damaged Alan inadvertently through the agency had presented too fine a moral point for him to grasp. He saw it now. I've betrayed him, he thought in anguish. My beloved brother – I'm not fit to live!

'And Sarah and her letter . . . These friends of yours, I suppose, did away with Colonel Ahmed.'

'I don't understand much about it, but I think Colonel Ahmed had been getting in their way and they wanted something to start the show off.'

'So you agreed to get rid of Sarah.'

'It wasn't like that, Mr Crawe,' he cried. But this part of his story was the most difficult of all to tell. He couldn't possibly, he realised even as he plunged into it, tell Alan exactly what had happened. So he faltered and improvised. His tongue played tricks with him, leading him into positions it became impossible to uphold without contradiction. He was not a good liar; his natural disposition was a frank and open one, and his lies were never cunning or well planned but sprang from the impulse of the moment, usually to protect a friend from unpleasant realities, or in extreme cases, to save his own skin. So in the end he gave himself away by his own evasions and inconsistencies.

Less than an hour after his release from jail the day before, Fakhr had rung him up. 'I simply can't go on,' he had told them. 'They'd suspect me now! You see the risk it would be!'

Fakhr had answered smoothly. 'Yes, of course, we understand. We'll put you on to something else. We'll get in touch with you in a day or two.' Knowing them, Ishmael had understood that he was being promoted into higher villainy. What would they ask of him now? What crimes, what murders did they have in store for him? Seized with despair he had awaited their instructions. And then, miraculously, a chance for escape came his way. When Sarah went that night to Alan's flat with her story of the letter and Colonel Ahmed, he saw his opportunity – that Colonel Ahmed should be sending messages to a high official of the Lebanese Security Police could have only one implication, and if Sarah delivered his letter, all the plans that Fakhr had so carefully prepared might go astray. And not only that – suppose the letter contained a reference to himself? He made up his mind then and there. After Sarah had gone he went to Fakhr and struck a bargain. If he handed her over to them, he said, would they leave him alone? They agreed, and what else could he do but trust them to keep their word when it was over.

Ishmael's voice faltered into silence. Humbly, he waited for Alan to pronounce judgement upon him. He was ready to accept whatever punishment his friend might prescribe for him. His political indiscretions had aroused terror, but no twinge of guilt in him. Why should he feel guilty? He owed nothing to the world but repayment in its own currency of grief and pain; but he had betrayed his friend, the man to whom he owed his life, his prosperity, his happiness. No punishment could be too heavy for this crime. His mind, having grasped the notion of his own treachery, now magnified it, for if he was to suffer, then it was necessary for him to suffer greatly. He believed in heaven and hell, but not in purgatory. His imagination played upon a variety of striking penances. I shall cut off my right hand, he thought, the hand that sealed the bargain with Fakhr. Or put it in a vice and crush it till the bones are broken. I shall cut out the tongue that led me into this treachery.

But still Alan kept his silence. The taxi driver, sitting on his stone, coughed and spat into the dust. Ishmael looked at him in surprise and saw that around them on the hills the shadows had lengthened. Long thin clouds, burnished into a shining gold, hung stretched out over the mountain ridges. He had not noticed the advance of the afternoon and the slanting golden light looked strange to him, as though he had wakened from an afternoon sleep and looked outside to see that time had passed over him. Fear, not of Alan and the Lebanese police, but of God, touched Ishmael.

He spoke, to break the silence. 'Mr Crawe, what are you going to do?'

Alan knew that Ishmael's big soft eyes were gazing at him, imploring for a kind word, a gesture of understanding, but he could not bear to look at him. He said coldly, 'We'll have to go and get her.'

'You can't do that! They'll kill you! You must believe me. They only want to keep her quiet so that she can't take that fellow's letter.'

Alan looked around him at the silent hills. They seemed cruel and revengeful, blistered with sunlight and scarred by dark wounds of shadow. It seemed to him that Sarah might well be dead. 'Where is she?'

'At Ain Houssaine, in the house next to the church. It belongs to a fellow called Jemali. It's much the best thing to just leave her there. You haven't got a chance of getting her out on your own.'

'Ishmael, get in the taxi. He'll take you back to Baalbek. I don't know what's going to happen over the next few days;

you'll have to manage on your own. Go to Beirut. Get out of here on the first plane you can get hold of, you and Georgette. You're always talking about opening a London office. Well, now we'll have to think about it seriously. If I don't see you before you go, I'll write to you at the London bank. I advise you to get out as quickly as you can.'

Poor England, he thought, God help it! The great garbage-can, the repository for all the world's rubbish, anyone too silly or soft to stick it out at home. As if it hasn't enough troubles, and now, on top of them all, Ishmael.

'Oh, Mr Crawe!' Ishmael nearly sobbed with relief. He wanted to throw his arms around his friend's neck and embrace him, but restrained himself. Experience had taught him that it was unwise in moments such as these to fuss around his friend with too many apologies and too much gratitude. 'What are you going to do?'

'I'm going on to find that wretched girl and bring her back. I knew she'd be trouble the first moment I saw her. Do you know I think she's actually in love with that dead man. Anyway she's my responsibility and I have to find her.'

'But you can't Mr Crawe, you simply can't. This car won't take that road. You'd have to have a jeep. Besides you're not armed and they are living in an arsenal. And what about those people in Baalbek? There are five of them and only one of her. If they kicked up a fuss or went to the press, you'd be finished. Come back with me and calm them down. Tell them anything. Tell them it was a case of life and death and when they see she isn't there, they'll believe you.'

'You're probably right,' said Alan slowly. 'We'll go back to Baalbek and phone the police.'

'No, no, Mr Crawe, only the Embassy as a last resort. And it isn't that yet. Georgette and I have to get away first. We'll catch the eleven-thirty plane. It's hardly ever full.' He had taken over. It was Alan who faltered and compromised. 'You read what that fellow said. Look, it isn't only the letter which they've probably got hold of by now. She's their hostage. That's why she's perfectly safe, and why she has to be safe. I think Fakhr isn't sure whether or not Colonel Ahmed is alive. If he is they'll swap her for him. She's English Mr Crawe. And so are you. If you went up there they'd have two aces in their hands.'

'I see Ishmael,' said Alan dryly. 'You are better informed than I am.'

'You don't have to be informed. It's common sense.'

The taxi driver shouted at them. Alan had forgotten him and was surprised to see him again seated at the wheel. He started up and set off rattling down the Beka'a.

CHAPTER 13

As the sun sank westward over the mountains the shadow of the escarpment crept forward across the valley, turning Lake Houssaine to a dull, slate grey and stilling the play of its waters. On the far side of the valley the sun still lingered, striking warm rose red on hills so bare that the few features that adorned them – a thorn bush, a white boulder, a contorted almond tree – became significant and mysterious as though inhabited by deities.

In Joseph Jemali's house the hens and the goat had been taken in for the night. The town was quiet; and in the silence the spring that gushed out from a chasm in the hillside above the town and plunged down into the lake lent a solemn note to the Ain Houssaine dusk.

With the coming of darkness Sarah began to feel the boredom of captivity. She paced the room impatiently and at length, to pass the time, opened the bottle of wine that Joseph Jemali had sent to her. The first glass revived her spirits so she took another and eventually finished it. Feeling drowsy and rather stupid she lay down on the divan and went to sleep.

The effects of the wine did not entirely work off until the following morning and perhaps contributed in some measure to the feeling she was to have of this night's strangeness. She seemed, alternatively, to wake and dream; to move through a world invaded by fantasies, through a darkness intermittently lit by curious images, the most vivid of which later seemed the least credible.

She awoke suddenly, and lay in the pitch dark conscious that the door was open. She could feel the cold air blowing in on her. A sound like the heavy breathing of an animal came to her ears and she started up fearing that something had come into her room and was snuffling toward her.

Then someone whispered, very close to her ear, 'Silence, *taisez-vous!*' And a hand touched her shoulder.

She caught her breath. Her eyes were becoming accustomed to the darkness. She saw the figure of a man outlined in the doorway. Another man bent over her and, feeling for her hand, drew her to her feet. *'Taisez! Taisez!'*

She could not see the face of either man, but the stealth and silence of their entry into the room and their whispered words reassured her. She followed them with perfect trust. It was flight, for her, into darkness with two figures as obscure as angels. They led her to the door. On the verandah, the beast that had frightened her turned out to be Joseph Jemali, snoring.

They crossed the courtyard – the two men moving soundlessly. As they reached the steps leading down onto the road, there was a snort, as sleepers sometimes make upon waking. They ran down the steps. Sarah stumbled and they lifted her up so that she fled along between them, her feet hardly touching the ground. It was an extraordinary and pleasing sensation. She floated like a ballerina skimming on the tips of her toes, but faster, faster. She was to remember not having run from Ain Houssaine, but having flown like a bird out of it.

They reached the outskirts of the town, where the spring cast its foaming torrents into a pool of darkness; a path led up the steep slope alongside it. Sarah caught the sting of ice-cold spray on her face and her ears were deafened by the roar of falling waters. The din confused her and it seemed to her that the town from which they had escaped had broken into shouting.

They hurried on up the hill, feeling their way round damp boulders and over rivulets that had broken away from the main body of the stream and gushed down to the lake in torrents of their own. The two men glided on their sure mountain feet, like cats that can see in the dark, for their pace hardly slackened as they ran light-foot over stepping stones, lifting Sarah between them. She kept her eyes on the path and at first did not see that there were other men nearby. Then someone spoke to them and they passed close to a boulder where a man crouched, rifle in hand. Suddenly, over to their right, came the sound of a report and a livid tongue of fire flashed out in the dark. Shots rang out below, and all around the hillside burst into answering fire.

Sarah's two escorts paid no heed but continued on up the mountain. It was lighter as they came out of the valley and the moon was about to rise. Over the crest of the hills the sky was thin like silver gauze. They could see the grim cliffs ahead, the contorted shapes of thorn bushes and boulders with flat, slanting sides like gigantic flints, as though some ancient race had fashioned stone heads for their spears, and had passed away, leaving these huge flakes of stone as evidence of their industry.

Suddenly, although all this time she had hardly put foot to the ground, Sarah felt exhausted. 'I'm tired, I must stop and rest.' The two men paid no heed, but carried her on up the hill.

They joined a road paved with big blocks of cut stone and edged by a rough stone wall. The moon rose, flooding the road, the valley and all the surrounding hills with clear, cold light. Sarah could see the way now. She looked at the rough wall and the worn surface of the stones beneath her feet. She thought, This is an old road. It must be the Emperor Domitian's road leading from Akfa to Ain Houssaine.

They were walking more slowly. The two men talked in low voices. Sarah, stupefied with exhaustion, allowed herself to be dragged between them. Once she looked down to see, lying on a stone in front of her and clear in the moonlight, a single full-blown rose, but this seemed too extraordinary, there was not a rosebush in sight. She put it down to imagination.

Soon after this they met the pilgrims; a great company of men and women, chanting and singing. They wore a strange dress that Sarah had not seen before; the women carried torches high above their heads; their long black hair hung unbound and was garlanded with red anemones. 'Adonis! Adonis!' they shrieked. Their eyes flashed white in the moonlight, like the eyes of wild animals. The men carried in their hands, above their heads, their severed and bleeding members, and they too shouted, 'Adonis! Adonis!' And so immersed were these beautiful, bloodstained people in the intoxication of their pilgrimage that they did not notice Sarah and her two rescuers, who slipped past them into the night.

The singing died away behind them and the flare of the torches disappeared as a bend in the road hid them from view.

In the silence that followed the moonlight was brighter on the ancient road. Sarah remembered that pilgrims had not passed that way for many hundreds of years.

She felt that they had been walking half the night when at last they came to Chakra. The moonlight showed a white church – the minaret of a mosque like a tall white pencil against the dark cliff behind. People came running to meet them. She heard shouting and laughter.

They came to a square. She was being led into a house. People clustered around her.

In Emile Khalife's house Sarah sat wrapped up in rugs, drinking coffee. The room was full of people – women were going in and out carrying trays of food, men wearing cartridge bandoliers and carrying rifles strode importantly about. Most of these people came up to Sarah and looked at her and spoke to her gently and respectfully. They brought her more coffee, another blanket . . . they offered her arak, olives, a basket of fat green figs.

She was their heroine, their saint, their special blessing. In days to come they would light candles for her in the church and put flowers on wayside shrines in her name. How she had served them they did not quite know. They did not really care to go into this; they simply accepted her. She had set out to save them from bloodshed. She had been captured by their old enemies; she had endured untold terror and suffering. They hovered about her looking with admiration at her blue eyes and milky skin. They remembered their Frankish ancestor, the beautiful Christian girl whose name the Chakra-Ain Houssaine feud had begun.

Emile Kahlife was a broad fat man whose belly when he laughed shook up and down like a half filled sack of wheat. Often when he didn't laugh, he chuckled, a deep husky sound that seemed to travel up from the soles of his feet and emerged much grated by its journey. His thick hair grew villainously close to his eyebrows, his moustache was abundant and tilted up into a waxed finish; but unmarked skin and the clarity of his eyes led Sarah to feel that she was looking at two men, imposed one upon the other, each fighting for preference.

Sarah was disconcerted to discover that on giving him his letter, he tucked it unopened in the purple sash that was bound several times around his waist. They both sat down on low, rush covered chairs, which with two wide divans spread with camel hair rugs were the only furniture. The room was lit by a kerosene lamp that flickered shadows on the whitewashed walls.

It was a large room, similar to the one she had occupied in Ain Houssaine, with two arches overlooking the village square. A third arch led into another room, dimly lit and guarded by a man squatting down and holding a rifle.

Emile Khalife asked Sarah how she had been treated in Ain Houssaine. 'They were kind but at first I was rather frightened.'

'Mountain people lose their heads at times. Probably the altitude.' He chuckled and his belly flopped up and down. He touched his moustache, which Sarah felt was a stage prop and could be taken off and put on as he wished. 'But on the whole they are hospitable people. Jemali isn't such a bad fellow.'

He stood up and said, 'I hope you will be comfortable here. You need some rest and it is still a few hours before dawn. Don't go into that room. There is a man there. He is seriously ill and he must not be disturbed.'

In a small room leading off her own, a doctor was attending to the wounded man. Every now and again she could hear the low murmur of his voice. She did not turn to look at this room, but was never forgetful of it; on the extreme edge of her vision she could see the open door and the light burning within.

After the doctor had left, Emile Khalife instructed Sarah again not to disturb the sick man, then he too left, and Sarah was alone.

She waited a little and then, taking off her shoes and carrying the lamp, went quietly into the next room and knelt down beside his bed. The guard sitting in a corner with a rifle by his side was asleep. So was Raschid. Sarah lifted the lamp and studied his face. I couldn't remember, she thought, and who could? So many gods and goddesses hovered in the Lebanese skies, it needed only a fractional shift of thought to believe in them. She put her hand on his forehead, lightly, so as not to awaken him, and discovered a short white scar, partly covered by his hair. An imperfection. He would not fade away in a twist of smoke. She bent down and kissed him.

A slight contraction of the muscles of his lips might have been a response. He opened his eyes, still foggy with sleep, and blinked twice to clear his vision; then shook his head as though to assemble his thoughts.

'Sarah, what are you doing here?'

'What you told me to do. I've delivered your letter to Mr Khalife.'

He put his hand on her wrist and smiled.

'But I don't suppose it matters any more.' She stood up but he gripped her hand.

He said, 'Don't go. Stay with me.'

Sarah brought cushions and camel hair rugs and put them down by his bed. He lay on his side and every now and again put out his hand and touched her face.

Sarah thought, He won't remember this, then she slept and dreamed. She was the principal boy in a pantomime. She wore a tight-fitting green jacket with a short skirt, like a ballet dancer's, standing out around her hips, sparkling with silver thread. She wore green glass slippers. She was in a cave lit by torches in sconces on the walls. Around her were large trunks with domed lids. Some of the lids were open and strings of emeralds, diamonds and rubies hung down from the sides of the trunks. Inside the trunks gold coins glittered when she held them in her hands and fell with a rushing sound, as she dropped them.

Then she saw a hand just above her head, holding a rope of pearls. The hand dropped the pearls around her throat and disappeared.

The torches died and Sarah was alone in the darkness of her sleep.

She awoke lying on the divan in the other room and wondered where the dream had begun.

The car moved slowly for the land was rough. Emile drove, Sarah beside him; Raschid sat in the back, supported by cushions.

'How are you getting on back there? Is this a bit rough for you?'

Sarah turned her head to catch his reply. Raschid saw the curve of her cheek and a lock of hair tucked behind her ear. He made no reply. 'He's asleep,' said Emile.

As they reached the Beka'a, the first signs of dawn were showing in the sky and the ridges of the anti-Lebanon stood out against a band of luminous pallor. Between them and these mountains expanded a sea of grey obscurity, but as the light increased, the ancient land slowly put on its features. Emile Khalife yawned. 'The day,' he said, 'of the revolution.'

'Well, I don't want to know about the revolution,' said Sarah. 'As long as you stop it and people don't get killed, that's all that matters. What I want to know is –'

'But, Mademoiselle, you have supported the government,' broke in Emile. 'You are on our side.'

'I'm not,' said Sarah. 'I'm just against violence.' This in fact summed up her political convictions; revolutions interrupted the natural happy course of life and men got killed who might otherwise have stayed alive so that women could love them. 'What I want to know,' she said, 'is –'

'Ah! Mademoiselle,' Emile interrupted her. 'You have a lot to learn about us. You think that because we arrest a few spies and confiscate a few rifles that violence has been stopped. Revolution is a great ball rolling around the Middle East. We do not stop it, we merely dodge out of its way. It is probably rolling off to Jordan now, or up to Iraq.'

Emile, in spite of his lighthearted tone, was worried. He had little relish for the business ahead. The tables might yet be turned. He had no intention of compromising himself by giving unnecessary information to a headstrong young woman.

So it was not until some weeks later that Sarah learned what had happened to Raschid after he had been shot down in Rue Zahle.

Raschid had regained consciousness shortly after he had

been taken to hospital; and even in those first hazy moments his most distinct thoughts were of Sarah. This was perhaps not surprising. The world had darkened around her face; her compassionate gaze had pursued him into oblivion and, awakening now out of it, he saw her face again, as though it had never left him.

For a long time his thoughts did not even touch upon his own hazardous position. He had escaped death, but something much more important than mere escape had happened to him, for in doing so he had collided with his destiny.

His nature dealt largely in extremes and the hours he had passed with Sarah came back to him. He told himself that no other woman had meant anything to him and that in their short meeting were the seeds of a lifetime's happiness. The idea, once having taken hold of his mind, possessed it. He had not simply fallen in love. His whole life had put on new colours.

A nurse came into his room, and with her a man wearing the uniform of the Lebanese Police. A little older than himself, thought Raschid, and a man who looked alert and intelligent. But Raschid did not know him for a friend or foe and evaded a number of his questions.

Some men had shot at him from a car, he told the inspector. He did not know who they were or why they had wanted to kill him.

'Where were you going? What were you doing in Rue Zahle?' the inspector asked him.

'I was visiting Colonel Mahumud Yazid of the Syrian Trade Mission.' They had had an appointment, he explained, to discuss the proposals they were going to put up to the Lebanese.

'Someone must have known of this appointment,' the inspector suggested. 'They must have been already waiting for you.'

'Possibly.'

'Do you have enemies in this country?' the inspector asked him.

Raschid watched him with half closed eyes. 'Not that I know of.'

'Lebanon is small. Perhaps you have enemies in other neighbouring countries.'

'If so, I know nothing of them.'

'This, Colonel, implies more than one.'

'It was you, Inspector, who implied more than one.'

'In spite of what you have been through, Colonel, you seem to have a clear mind.'

'The wounds in my shoulder and thigh are of no great matter.'

'But the wound in your chest, so your doctor told me, was close to your heart and could have killed you.'

Raschid smiled. 'But it didn't. I've been very lucky. And I think the man or men who shot me realised this or they would not have come back.'

'Concerning Mr Yazid, you did not come to Lebanon together?'

'He came three days before me. He had relatives to see.'

'And you also have a brother in Beirut?'

Raschid made no reply, and the inspector continued the interrogation, asking questions that came alarmingly close to the bone.

'My friend, I love Syria. I do not want to spend the rest of my life in exile wandering round Europe from one casino to another – you mistake my character if you think my ambitions lie in that line. I understand that the Lebanese would like nothing better than for me to make accusations against my country. I can imagine what is happening – they are saying you killed me. Is that it? My body is to be used as a bridge to the next uprising. Well, let them tread over me. I am not dead yet. Do you imagine that because I am used unjustly, I shall fly to your protection like any traitor? What good would it do if you waved my confessions in the face of the world? My people would turn against me; they would say I have sold myself to the Lebanese. As for Colonel

Yazid, they would make a martyr of him. And what should I see then of Syria? Tell your politicians that if they use me in that way I shall denounce them throughout Arabia.' He turned away and closed his eyes.

The inspector, alarmed, hastened to reassure him. 'It is our earnest wish to protect you, to seek out the assassins. Naturally, Colonel, it is my duty to question you.'

But Raschid continued to lie with closed eyes – deaf to further questions.

After the inspector had gone, he slept and when he awoke again it was to find Tawfik by his bedside.

The two brothers smiled at each other. There was a great sympathy between them, though their lives had taken very different directions.

'This was kind of them,' said Raschid, 'to send you to me. Or has it been published in the press that I am here?'

'Not a word. The people think you are dead and Radio Cairo supports that. I knew nothing until they rang me from the hospital, at two o'clock, you had just regained consciousness. They said you asked for me and I came straightaway, but you were sleeping and they would not let me stay.'

'Did I ask for you? I don't remember. I am sorry, Tawfik.'

'How can you say that?' Tawfik looked at him reproachfully. It was acknowledged between them that he was nervous of his younger brother's career and troubled by a constant fear that it might damage his own. 'I would have stayed and watched you, but they would not let me. They told me to come again this evening and so I have come.'

'Is it evening?' Raschid turned his head to the window and saw that the sky had darkened to an intense violet.

Tawfik leaned forward and spoke with deep emotion. 'Raschid, this is a terrible thing. A terrible thing!'

Raschid smiled. 'I should have thought it a most happy occasion. I am well. I am safe. How are Alexa and the children? Are they well?'

'We have taken a house in Dour-esh-Chouer this year;

they're going up next weekend. The youngest boy is at school now, you know. Do not put me off, Raschid! I beg you. Think of the last time! Why do you put yourself in such a position? Why are you a man to be shot at? Come to me, I implore you! There will always be a place for you in my business. It is prosperous; it can support you. You can live with us. Alex has always been fond of you.'

Raschid shook his head. 'I cannot accept, Tawfik. Can you see me selling suit lengths to fat Armenians and Maronites?'

Tawfik suppressed his indignation. 'I can do it,' he said. 'There is no loss of dignity in honest business. Think of us. You are my only brother. And what are you achieving? You call yourself a patriot. Is it patriotism to lie bleeding in the gutter?'

Raschid regarded his brother sombrely. 'We are a bungling and ineffectual people, Tawfik. Even our assassinations misfire; and we are so divided that even as I point my gun at our deadliest enemy, the friend at my side jolts my elbow in case too much credit falls to me.'

'You mean that Colonel Yazid?'

'I think so.'

'But why?'

'I have known for some time that he wants me out of the way. He has an unsympathetic character. He holds a high rank, but he is not liked. He has little power and he's looking for power elsewhere.'

'Stop Raschid. I do not want to hear any more.'

'But you must listen to me. If I die, someone must know, and it is better he should be uninvolved. The Lebanese are being led, or forced, you might say, into an insurrection, and I believe that Yazid is behind this. What is more he knows that I know, and that is why he tried to kill me. He is smuggling arms into this country which are being dispersed in a number of remote villages. He is fostering old village feuds. He is a dangerous man and he must be stopped.'

'So are you going to arrange for his assassination? Where will this end?'

'Tawfik, all I want is that he should be exposed. The people of our countries must not be allowed to admire such a man.'

'This is a dirty business Raschid, and you are living in an open trench.'

'This fell upon me by chance. Would you have expected me to forget it? I have no further interest in what you call this dirty business. I am approaching forty. It is time for me to marry and raise a family.'

'I don't believe it. This fever is in your blood, and you have known too many women to settle down with one.'

Raschid smiled. 'Wait and see.'

'Raschid, in this life you are surrounded by betrayal and deceit. This girl whom you trusted has betrayed you.'

Raschid spoke softly, raising his head from his pillow to look into his brother's eyes. 'What do you mean?'

'I have seen her. I came here this afternoon, as I told you. You were sleeping. They said your condition was not serious but that you must rest, so I left and set out to do as you had asked me. I went to the bank and drew out the money and then I went to the girl's house at the address you gave me. I did not go in for I thought that someone might be watching me. I waited till she came out and then I followed her. I gave her the money and she took it.' He dropped his voice to a whisper. 'Had she some commission to carry out?'

'Yes.'

'I knew it! She took your money but pretended to know nothing. She was afraid. She saw your danger and now she is looking after her own skin and robbing you at the same time. Why do you trust this woman? Can she do you any harm?'

'No. It's I who could harm her. I have asked too much of her.'

'She has gone. She has left Beirut. I wondered if I had misjudged her and went to the house where she has been staying. The two old people who own the house told me that she would be away for a while. There you see?'

'I see. But you don't, Tawfik.'

'You're tired. I'll go.'

When he had gone, Raschid lay considering his plans. Sarah's presence pervaded the room.

The doctor, a humorous Scotsman, came to see him. The nurses dressed his wounds.

When they had gone, he waited a few minutes then sat up, threw back the blanket and slowly got himself out of bed. With the supreme contempt for his own weakness and pain that had marked his ancestors, he dressed. His torn, bloodstained jacket had been taken away so he tucked his pyjama jacket into his trousers and, pulling a blanket from the bed, wrapped it around his shoulders. Supporting himself with a hand on the wall, he made his way down the hospital corridor. It was the time for visitors.

He came to the stairs and descended them slowly. He avoided the main entrance, knowing he would be stopped there, and looked along the corridor of the ground floor for a way out. He found a door leading into the garden and opened it. He did not think of the pain as an ordeal to be endured, only as an enemy to be mastered. Concentrating all his will, he dragged himself across the garden to a side gate. A few steps further on and he had reached a busy road. A taxi cruised by. He hailed it and, falling into the back, gasped, 'Take me to Chakra.'

The words were hardly spoken when he fainted, but he regained consciousness some moments later to find himself passing the museum and the Roman columns of Fourn-ech-Chebbak. A little further on, as the land began to slant toward the mountains, he saw the first police trap on the road ahead and, suspecting that there would be more on the Damascus road, told the driver to turn aside and drive over the mountains by a lesser known way. It was a long and painful journey, for the winding village roads were still potholed from the winter rains and blocked here and there by landfalls from the cliffs above.

They reached Chakra at four in the afternoon.

CHAPTER 14

———

During the following weeks Beirut hovered, indecisively, between peace and revolution. In spite of the government's swift action in arresting the ringleaders, a good many troublemakers managed to disappear underground and, although quantities of arms had been seized all over the country, enough remained in circulation to make life alarming. A curfew was imposed and police patrolled the streets day and night, but outbursts of firing and isolated explosions took their toll. At the beginning of the second week the casualty list stood at fifteen.

The people, although accustomed in a measure to this kind of situation, avoided the centre of Beirut. In any case most of the shops were closed and there was no reason for going there. Though never entirely empty, the streets had a desolate appearance and, with fewer taxis trying to pass each other three abreast, were seen to be wider than one had imagined. People who ventured out were conscious of a feeling of isolation and heard a silence which, in this usually noisy city, overcame sound.

Only in the swimming clubs was the crisis forgotten. These places, like Jupiter's temple, imposed their own conditions upon their devotees. From the jewel-clear water, the salt-white, corrugated cliffs and the gardens of bright umbrellas, emanated an atmosphere of irrepressible and remorseless gaiety that reduced the agitations of Beirut as the sun fades into invisibility the light of a candle. Summer had come, people had to swim – it was a natural law and all else bowed before it. There was no falling off in attendance. If anything, the Lebanese, bereft of other amusements, thronged more eagerly to the sea's edge, which would perhaps indicate that their troubles were but superficial – flesh wounds that would quickly heal.

As they drove off the Corniche into the parking lots they talked excitedly about the latest rumours – the politician who had been arrested the night before, the cache of arms in the Phoenician tomb at Byblos, the news from Damascus of a split in the Syrian army . . . But when they left their cars and walked out onto the terrace by the changing rooms, these words died upon their lips. The sun, falling across the blue water, struck blindingly, cleansingly, upon their faces; and their acres faded, leaving them open to the impression of white spray and coloured umbrellas, of green weed swirling upon a rock, the turn of a bird's wing, the smile of a friend.

The second week of the crisis showed an improvement and the situation became more stable as feeling within Lebanon began to swing in the government's favour. The general strike, at all times threatening, had never quite become a reality. The Lebanese could resign themselves to bloodshed and the boycotting of certain areas, but not to the utter dislocation of trade, with the docks at a standstill and the airport closed, and they were grateful to the government for having saved them, in the nick of time, from this supreme disaster.

The atmosphere was further improved when a number of the men who had been arrested were pardoned. The supporters of Salem Farid, for instance, were thought to have had a genuine grievance, and anyone who could claim kinship with the exiled politician was set free. This pleased not only the opposition, but also government supporters, who were glad to know that they could still go in for this kind of thing without undue fear of being punished for it. For who could tell, maybe in the elections next year they might be forced to use unorthodox methods themselves.

But the crisis was overcome in the long run simply by people becoming bored with it. When everyone had been either frightened or angry there had been no time to ask what it was all about, but with passions cooling the question seemed suddenly irrelevant – and no adequate answer was forthcoming. Even Radio Cairo seemed to feel it was wasting its breath, and, after one final, impassioned broadcast on a Thursday afternoon, dropped Lebanon, and threw its weight into a campaign advocating the assassination of King Hussein. As for the Syrians, they had become occupied with troubles in Damascus – a struggle for power within the army had come to a head and several senior officers were arrested.

One afternoon about three weeks after the shooting of Colonel Ahmed, Nadea returned to her apartment to find Sarah sitting on the verandah, her skirt pulled up to her knees and her legs stretched out to catch the sun.

Nadea had been seeing off the Thornes, who had only that day left Beirut. They had been forced to postpone their departure, owing to a revival of interest in the Sofar affair. The escaped driver, it turned out, had been found hiding in a mountain village, and on his arrest had declared that Nigel Thorne had instructed him to put the guns in the back of the car. Naturally these accusations had to be checked. Nothing could be proved, but nothing could be disproved either . . . and so the days went by. Nigel found himself confronted by some articles he had written for an English weekly, expressing opinions about Egypt, Syria and Lebanon which, in his present situation, were an embarrassment. Only intervention at high levels finally persuaded the Lebanese of his innocence.

'Poor things,' Nadea remarked. 'They didn't like it here.

They didn't have a good word to say for us. And what did you do to them, Sarah? I gave Margaret your message but she sounded awfully cold. You seem to have rubbed her up the wrong way.'

'There was a mix-up that day in Baalbek,' said Sarah. 'They were left without a car.'

'Don't I know it! It seems to have upset her more than anything else. She kept harping on about some objectionable Iranian.'

Sarah smiled. She was sorry that Margaret had left disliking her. She would have liked to have explained. But she had not explained to anyone – not even to Nadea.

'Well,' said Nadea, 'I'm going swimming now. Are you coming?' She put the question as a matter of form, knowing what the answer would be.

Sarah shook her head.

'What's the matter with you?' Nadea broke out impatiently. 'You've hardly been out of the house for the past week.'

'I'm saving money.'

'Good God! I'll pay!'

'I can't sponge on you forever.'

'You sponged on me for three months when you first came here and didn't turn a hair. What's the matter with you? You hang around here all day painting your toenails and rubbing oil on your legs.' She frowned at Sarah suspiciously. 'You're not waiting for Marcel to turn up again, are you? Well, if you want to know he's been at the swimming club all last week, so if you want to see him . . .'

'All the more reason for staying away.'

'He's been with that blonde, but you can see he's fed up with her. He came over to me yesterday and asked after you.'

'You don't want me to go back to Marcel, do you?'

'God forbid! But you worry me. There you go again with that smile. What have you got to smile about?'

'Darling Nadea, do go off and don't bother me.' She

leaned back in her chair and stretched out her feet to the verandah railing. I ought to go with her, she thought. But the prospect held no temptation. A delicious lethargy enfolded her. Nadea left, and she settled herself deeper into her chair, smiling freely now.

In the apartment across the road the fat man in pyjamas leaned over the balcony eating a slice of watermelon. Seeing Sarah's smile, he returned it. She frowned; he watched her for a moment hopefully, but eliciting no response lazily scratched an armpit and turned away.

'Sarah!' Nadea had returned. 'There's someone here to see you.'

'Who?' But she had already seen the tall figure standing behind Nadea. Hastily pulling down her skirt, she got up.

Colonel Ahmed bowed gravely. He wore a light grey suit and a blue silk tie dotted with red roses. A barber had recently shaved him and cut his hair. He had lost weight and his eyes, beneath their beautifully defined straight brows, burned with a residue of sickness. Sarah stood looking at him dumbly.

'Please sit down,' said Nadea, breaking the silence.

They sat down. Raschid was the first to speak.

'Perhaps you did not know that I was still in Beirut.'

'Yes, I knew.'

'You did not come to see me in hospital.'

Sarah smiled but made no reply.

'Every day I expected you.'

'As Sarah is apparently not going to introduce us,' said Nadea, 'I shall introduce myself. I am Nadea Raziyah.'

He stood up and bowed. 'Nadea, this is Colonel Ahmed,' said Sarah.

'Good God, you're the man who was shot in Rue Zahle!' cried Nadea, and burst into excited Arabic.

'Sarah, you didn't tell me you knew Colonel Ahmed.' Now they were both staring at her, intently.

Sarah smiled. 'It slipped my mind.' Colonel Ahmed drew in his breath softly and fixed her with a glowing regard.

'Would you like some coffee?' asked Nadea.

'Yes, thank you, please.' He waited till Nadea had gone and then, leaning forward, declared softly, 'Not a letter did you write, neither did you send me flowers. I expected a letter.'

'I thought about it,' said Sarah. 'But I decided that if I went to see you or wrote to you or sent you flowers, you would say I had put you at a disadvantage.'

He looked at her uncertainly. 'You are laughing at me.'

'Never!'

'It is so,' he said sadly. 'That is how I remember you.'

Sarah thought in panic, What have I done? I've offended him. This was not how she remembered him – his handsome mouth sulky, his low brows drawn. Nevertheless, she realised now, this was how he had been.

'No Muslim woman,' she said, 'would have done such a thing. You'd think it immodest. Now admit it!'

'You are not a Muslim woman!' Suddenly, decisively, he stood up. 'I want to talk to you but not here in front of your friend.'

When Nadea returned they had gone.

CHAPTER 15

Raschid drove at high speed into Avenue Bliss and down the hill toward the Bain Militaire. Here he slowed down and cruised along the Corniche.

The Bain Militaire was festive with splashing swimmers. A man in pink shorts and a wide-brimmed straw hat fished from the rocks; the water was dotted with bright bathing caps; small boys dived or jumped from the high board and swam about effortlessly.

Raschid followed the winding road along the contours of bays and peninsulas. Above Pigeon Rock he stopped at one of the cafés, overlooking the sea. He chose a table at the cliff's edge and, while he talked to a waiter, Sarah sat, bathed in sunlight, happiness and confusion.

When the waiter had gone she said, 'Aren't you afraid that someone will shoot at you? Or throw a bomb?'

'Look around you. See how quiet it is.'

Sarah obediently looked at a vine hung with clusters of purple grapes, pink oleanders in pots, and two white cuttle-fish canoes darting towards the tunnel in Pigeon Rock.

'Is it quiet because your colleague, Colonel Yazid, was assassinated last week?'

'Why do you say that?'

'It seems so strange. Two Syrian colonels assassinated within a month or so. Do you know who killed him?'

Raschid's face became grim and angry. 'I do not! The

Middle East is clamorous with conflicting ideals and opinions. Is it any wonder that sometimes we stumble over one another?'

'What will you do now? Return to Syria?'

'Of course. It is my home.'

'You know, I have always thought of Syria as being an empty land covered in sand hills.'

Raschid laughed and Sarah thought how unpredictable he was. She had expected him to be angry.

After a while the waiter reappeared with a mezzeh, which was enormous; olives, tabouli, homus, grilled chicken, capsicum stuffed with spiced tomato, aubergine stuffed with pine nuts and rice. There was hardly room on the table for the array of dishes. Twelve people, thought Sarah, could have made a feast of it. What a ridiculous display. The pink car all over again. For the first time she noticed the roses on his tie.

'Will you begin please. I cannot eat before you and I am ravenous,' said Raschid.

'I'm not at all hungry,' said Sarah. 'I don't want anything.'

'But I have ordered this for you.'

'No you haven't. You've ordered it for yourself. You don't seem to understand that I am not an appendage to a man, to be trailed along and do as I'm told. I never eat in the afternoon. I would like coffee please and a glass of water.' Whatever made me say that? Because his personality is so powerful and I am afraid of him? Yes; I am afraid.

Colonel Ahmed shouted at the waiter, glared at Sarah and, dipping his fingers into the dishes around him, began to eat wolfishly.

'You insult me by refusing my hospitality.'

'All right,' said Sarah, almost in tears. 'I insult you. There's nothing new in that.'

Colonel Ahmed again shouted at the waiter, dipped his hands into a finger bowl and sulked until the mezzeh was taken away and the coffee arrived.

'You said you were ravenous.'

He made no reply.

'You haven't known many western women have you, Raschid?'

'On the contrary. I have known many.'

Sarah heard herself say, 'Did you make love to them?' Then waited, appalled, for his answer.

But he seemed unperturbed. 'Of course I did.' He pondered, giving the impression that the past years had been so fully occupied by amorous episodes, he had some difficulty in sorting them out.

'Was there anyone in particular?'

'No. Women in the West have won independence and power, but they have paid too high a price. I was a young man with plenty of money and I spent three years in England. A man who did not take advantage of this would hardly have been a man. As for western women, I found them hard and inflexible. Your modern painters draw women in angles and straight lines. Think of Picasso. When he looked at a woman, he saw a heap of scrap iron or a factory chimney. What artist in the past has ever drawn women in that way? The lines of their bodies flow like water and curve like fruit. That is how artists in the past have always painted them.'

'I know. But there's no point in complaining. That's the way we are now. You're fond of talking about history – well, this is what history has done to us. We can't go back to what we were. If you don't like us,' she cried angrily, 'then go back to your own women. There must be many beautiful women in Syria.'

The mezzeh and the bottles of beer had been taken away. He leaned across the table toward her and spoke swiftly in Arabic. His voice had the lilting beauty of that language in its softer moods.

Suddenly it seemed to Sarah that everything they had said had been meaningless – a deception to hide the mysterious accord that was between them.

'What did you say?'

'I said I do not want any woman but you, and I asked you to marry me.'

For some moments, neither spoke. Sarah's mind was blank and her body uncomfortably alive.

'You don't look at me,' said Raschid gently. 'Please look up. Let me see your eyes.'

Sarah complied but said nothing. 'Are you afraid?' he asked gently. 'I think you are afraid because you are English and I am Syrian.'

Sarah shook her head.

'Then you must be afraid because I am Muslim and you are Christian.'

'Perhaps.'

'What does it matter? There is one God for us all.'

'There. You've said it yourself. You talk of God and we don't. You pray in public, and we pray in private, if we pray at all, and most of us don't. We call ourselves Christians, but what we really mean is that we try to behave within a moral code that derives from Christianity and that requires us to look after the old, the sick and the poor. We give money to starving people, to the Salvation Army, to the blind, the hungry, and to people who have been mutilated by our wars. But we think of ourselves a great deal and believe we are thinking of others. For you he is a reality. For us he is a symbol of generosity and correct behaviour.'

Raschid listened to her attentively. 'This is a very complex subject, Sarah, and you're probably right. But what has it got to do with us? We aren't symbols. We're human beings. Now we must get a licence and find a church. We'll marry here in your church and then again in Damascus.' He took her hand and stood up, but Sarah remained seated.

'I haven't even said I will marry you.'

'Of course you have. Why do you make these stupid difficulties?'

'Isn't it the custom in your country to ask your father or the head of your family when you make a decision like this?'

'My father is dead. I don't like my uncle, and for me the head of my family is my mother, and I have already asked her."

'What did you say?'

'I said I want to marry an English girl because she is beautiful and brave and I want her in my bed.'

'When did you say this?'

'After the bomb exploded in the suk. When you were choosing a handbag.'

'Oh my God!'

Raschid roared with laughter.

'That's different. That's just letting off steam,' said Sarah stiffly. A short silence followed. 'Raschid, you are asking me to go with you to a foreign country where I don't know the language and haven't a single friend. And all I know about you is that you're the sort of man who gets shot at. I don't want to be a widow half an hour after I'm married.'

'I shall not be shot at when you are with me. This has already been proved. Now come along, before you think up something else.'

Sarah, still somewhat dazed, took his hand. She felt that the pink oleandas, the sparkling sea and the two white canoes darting towards Pigeon Rock now shone as though washed by celestial rain, with a brilliance they had never shown before. She lifted her face and knew that it was beautiful, like an offering. 'Of course I'll marry you. I adore you. I loved you the first moment I saw you.'

Raschid smiled. 'I shall give you my most precious possession. A dappled grey mare with a silver tail.' He looked at his watch. 'We must get your passport and a visa. We must hurry.'

'I've already done all that,' said Sarah. 'Mr Khalife helped me. Wasn't it kind of him?'

Raschid laughed. Sarah laughed.

They laughed and laughed.

THE END

AFTERWORD

Charlotte Jay was born Geraldine Mary Jay in 1919 in Adelaide, where she works under her married name, Geraldine Halls, as a writer and oriental art dealer. She grew up in Adelaide, attending Girton School (now Pembroke School) and the University of Adelaide. She worked as a secretary in Adelaide, Sydney, Melbourne and London during the 1940s and as a court stenographer for the (Australian) Court of Papua New Guinea during 1949. During the 1950s she and her husband, John, who worked for UNESCO, travelled and lived in Lebanon, Pakistan, Thailand, India and France. They operated an oriental art business in Somerset between 1958 and 1971, and since then, in Adelaide. (John died in 1982.)

Charlotte Jay is the name she used to publish most of her nine mystery novels. Except for *The Voice of the Crab* (1974), they were first published between 1951 and 1964 and reflect a life spent travelling and her fascination with local cultures and ethnological questions, as do her six 'straight' novels published as Geraldine Halls between 1956 and 1982. Only her first novel, *The Knife is Feminine*, is set in Australia. In others, the action takes place in Pakistan, Japan, Thailand, England, Lebanon, India, Papua New Guinea, and the Trobrian Islands. Most of her Charlotte Jay mysteries were first published by Collins in London and Harper in New York. They have appeared in various editions and have been translated around the world – *The Fugitive Eye* was made into a Hollywood movie starring Charlton Heston – but have not until now been published in Australia. She confesses she became rather confused about her national identity during her heyday as a mystery writer. The American reviewers always referred to her as British, the British reviewers called her an Australian, and the Australian reviewers more or less ignored her. Something of Charlotte Jay's mixed identity might be reflected in Sarah Lane, the heroine of *Arms for Adonis*, a young British woman who 'felt she had been born in the wrong country and craved the sun'.

She has described her motives and methods as a mystery writer like this: 'I began writing mystery stories largely because of my delight in the novels of Wilkie Collins and Le Fanu and the stories of Poe. I read these books with terror and fascination when I was quite young and their influence can be seen in several of my early novels. When my first books were published most of the crime stories at that time were written by skilled writers of crime and detection, usually with a well-born ex-Oxford or Cambridge amateur as the private detective as the central character, appearing in the manner of the Scarlet Pimpernel, something of a fool, but omniscient and strides ahead of the reader. In America the same fashion prevailed along with crime stories following in the tradition of Dashiell Hammett and Raymond Chandler. I knew I could not compete with excellent exponents of these varied trends. Many had direct experience of police procedure which I did not feel confident of learning anything much about. And indeed I felt no interest in doing so. I set out to frighten my readers by asking them to identify themselves with a character battling for survival in a lonely, claustrophobic situation. My publishers on several occasions demanded that, in the interest of logicality, my threatened character should call the police. I always contested their suggestions and sometimes rewrote whole chapters to accommodate my conviction that my characters must stumble on alone and unaided through their private nightmares.' (From *Twentieth Century Crime and Mystery Writers*, St James Press, 1985).

Arms for Adonis was first published in 1961 by Collins (UK) and Harper (USA) and in 1962 as a paperback Collier Mystery Classic. Charlotte Jay has revised and in places rewritten the novel for publication in Wakefield Crime Classics. She wrote the book during the months leading up to the invasion of Egypt in 1956 by England, France and Israel (the Suez Crisis). She was living in Beirut during a one year 'tour of duty' by her husband, John, who was a senior official for the United Nations Relief and Works Agency in the Middle East. Her time was spent immersed in the history and atmosphere of Lebanon, a country she loved in a period of great happiness in her own life.

This tranquil, yet intense awareness is vividly and beautifully reflected in the sensual description of landscape. One of Charlotte Jay's skills is to give a scene, a setting, a country, a living presence (as in the evocations of jungle in *Beat Not the Bones*, Wakefield Crime Classics, 1992). Beirut and Lebanon are both minor protagonists in *Arms for Adonis*. Odd moments, snapshots, cameo portraits fill the opening chapter and they variously allow the reader to 'touch', 'smell', 'see' Beirut.

Later, the country's interior comes to life:

The broad green valley stretched away to north and south, and in front of them, surprisingly near, the long range of the Lebanon rose up like a barrier. These are extraordinary mountains, appearing from over the Beka'a both massive and delicate, their lower slopes intricately folded and pierced by innumerable valleys, their crests glittering with snow – not the abundant whiteness of winter, this had melted away – but summer snow like veins of silver struck down between the naked grey ridges.

The lower slopes were warm with sunshine; rocks and stones shone blinding white in the thin, clear air and almond and peach trees putting out new leaf trembled and shimmered as though green water was netted in their branches. But as they mounted higher the mood of the landscape became sad and threatening; huge ash-grey clouds moved swiftly down the mountain slopes blotting out the road ahead.

As they went higher, the mist thickened. The posts at the side of the road, grey boulders, thorn bushes, and almond trees black and twisted like corroded iron, appeared like spectres. A shepherd in a white keffiyeh and baggy trousers stood watching over them, a ghostly figure with the mist whirling around him.

These random instances represent Charlotte Jay's creative method in this book – the overwhelming use of the metaphorical trope of light and white, sometimes dazzlingly so. The device is brilliant and justified, because the story revolves around the Greek myth of Venus and Adonis (the Romans 'claimed' Venus as Aphrodite). The myth links the political thriller and the love strands of the story – Colonel Ahmed is Adonis; Sarah, Aphrodite. Alert readers should have picked the inevitability of their union for they were destined for one another. As Charlotte Jay commented in conversation with the editors, 'You cannot step out of a myth.' And why the Adonis myth? Let Charlotte Jay explain: 'Adonis is very important in Lebanon. You see, the Adonis river rises in Lebanon . . . although it is a Greek myth, somehow or other, Lebanon seems to have taken it to itself. You have the source of the Adonis and then about ten miles away, over the top of the mountains, there is a lake and it's said that the pilgrims from the Adonis festivals practised fertility rites when the males severed their penises and walked along the ancient Emperor Domitian's Road and threw themselves into the lake for purification.'

This aspect of Lebanon's mythic past is joltingly described in Sarah's vision during her escape from Äin Houssaine.

Arms for Adonis has been classed as a brilliant travel book – 'excellent scenery and local colour' (*Saturday Review*) and, tragically, it could be so read. 'Tragically' because Jay's Beirut and Lebanon no longer exist. (As we write this afterword in 1993, the Israeli army bombs the civilian population of Southern Lebanon.) Her lovely evocations represent lost journeys. Obviously, this travelogue view is only partly accurate. There are more important emphases.

The political aspect of the book needs no development here other than to point out Jay's sanity in her depictions of the crazy fluctuations and alliances in the Middle East. Her method is that of the skilled novelist, allowing her characters *in situ* to comment on the larger actualities, often with a wry, ironic humour. Much of the blame for every problem, then, was targeted at Britain, the cynical diplomatic manipulations of America and France being unremarked for the most part. Jay puts it neatly: 'in the Middle East . . . so much that was distressing to the humanitarian mind – the refugee camps in the Jordan valley, the devastated areas of Jerusalem where Jew had murdered Arab and Arab had murdered Jew, even purdah, beggars and the suspicions of the Syrian customs officials – could, if one felt so inclined, be laid at the door of British imperialism.' Britain has gone, but the wild switches of policy and emotions are no different now from what they were forty years ago. Jay does offer, however, a civilised, if wistful, solution to the chaos, one utterly devoid of political and international correctness and, therefore, likely to be derided by the mad political leaders of our era.

In the final analysis the book is about marriages, comings together, workable assimilations. Sarah's name is both Jewish and Muslim; St Joseph's Maronite church 'seems to embody the pagan temple, the mosque and the church – an oriental and Mediterranean synthesis'; Sarah (an Englishwoman) realises a 'mysterious and frightening accord that was between them' (between herself and Raschid Ahmed, a Syrian); Jay says of Beirut that 'it is both European and Asian and must perforce face both ways – or, at any rate, it cannot afford to alarm its own divided nature by looking too fixedly in one direction'.

These compromises are themselves part of the 'mystery' of the book, in which shifting commitments and liaisons represent the political and personal realities in a fictional and actual world which has no apparent fixed centre. That descriptions of the chaos can still satisfy the reader is a reflection of Charlotte Jay's skill and romantic optimism, probably the only sensible resolution of a story set in a strange and mad time.

PETER MOSS AND MICHAEL J. TOLLEY

WAKEFIELD CRIME CLASSICS

Peter Moss and Michael J. Tolley, general editors of the Wakefield Crime Classics series, are colleagues at the University of Adelaide. Late in 1988, they began assembling a series of Australian 'classic' crime fiction and soon realised that the problem was not going to be one of finding sufficient works of high quality, but of finding a bold enough publisher fired with the same vision.

This series revives forgotten or neglected gems of crime and mystery fiction by Australian authors. Many of the writers have established international reputations but are little known in Australia. In the wake of the excitement generated by the new wave of Australian crime fiction writers, we hope that the achievements of earlier days can be justly celebrated.

If you wish to be informed about new books as they are released in the Wakefield Crime Classics series, send your name and address to Wakefield Press, Box 2266, Kent Town, South Australia 5071, phone (08) 362 8800, fax (08) 362 7592.

Also available in

WAKEFIELD CRIME CLASSICS

A HANK OF HAIR
by Charlotte Jay

Gilbert Hand hasn't been the same since his wife died. He's moved to a dull but respectable hotel where silence seems to brood in the hall and stairway. In a secret drawer he discovers a long, thick hank of human hair, and his world narrows down to two people – himself and the murderer.

'Stark horror told as genteely as a bedtime story. Excellent nightmare reading.'
London *Evening Standard*

'Takes the reader in with the first sentence. All the succeeding sentences line up neatly, shudder to shudder.'
Duluth *News-Tribune*

'There *are* Draculas and there *are* Dracula victims.'
Charlotte Jay